The Alpha Plague 6

Michael Robertson

Website and Newsletter:
www.michaelrobertson.co.uk

Email: subscribers@michaelrobertson.co.uk

Edited by:
Terri King - http://terri-king.wix.com/editing
And
Pauline Nolet - http://www.paulinenolet.com

Cover Design by Christian Bentulan

Formatting by Polgarus Studio

The Alpha Plague 6
Michael Robertson
© 2017 Michael Robertson

The Alpha Plague 6 is a work of fiction. The characters, incidents, situations, and all dialogue are entirely a product of the author's imagination, or are used fictitiously and are not in any way representative of real people, places or things.

Any resemblance to persons living or dead is entirely coincidental.

All rights reserved

No part of this publication may be reproduced, stored in a retrieval system or transmitted in any form or by any means electronic, mechanical, photocopying, recording or otherwise, without the prior written permission of the author except in the case of brief quotations embodied in critical articles and reviews.

Would you like to be notified when I have a new release?
Join my mailing list for all of my updates here:-

www.michaelrobertson.co.uk

Chapter One

The long grass—still damp from the morning dew—whipped at Vicky's legs and dragged against her getaway as she fought to regulate her breaths. She'd made this run countless times already and she had the beating of them. Not that her heart got the message; it pounded in her chest as if trying to bash its way free.

"You're fucking insane, you know that?" Serj called at her from behind. His accusations usually started about now. Not quite as fast as Vicky, the panic often kicked in for him just before they reached the woods and he always took it out on her. He'd coped up until now and had been fine every other time, so she had no reason to believe he'd fail today.

"Yet *you* listen to me," Vicky called back to him, dragging a deep breath before she added, "so what does that say about you?"

The dense trees muffled Serj's reply as Vicky ducked into the woods, swerving through the tightly packed trunks with both Serj and the eight to twelve diseased behind her. They'd run this route so many times that Vicky went into autopilot and fell into her usual pattern of twisting and turning to navigate the mazy path.

The quick changes in direction dragged on Vicky's tired

limbs, and her legs shook from the extra effort. Every deep inhale pulled the pine-scented air into her lungs. It made sense to run through the trees because it gave them the edge. With better control over their bodies than the diseased, they could navigate the complex route more easily.

About halfway through the tight space, Vicky heard the diseased enter behind them. Clumsy footsteps crunched through the dead leaves on the ground, and screams followed thuds as they ran into tree after tree. In a different situation, it would have been funny to listen to.

When Vicky burst out of the woods on the other side, the strong sunlight dazzled her. She squinted against it, her eyes stinging, but she kept going. A second later, she heard Serj's heavy steps behind her, his fitness clearly waning.

No more than a hundred metres to go, Vicky looked at the huge oak tree that served as their destination. For some reason, the final stretch always felt the worst and Vicky dug deep to will her clumsy body forward.

Two thick ropes hung down from one of the tree's main branches. One for Vicky and one for Serj.

When Vicky looked behind again, she saw the pack of diseased emerge from the woods. They wore the same fury she'd seen on their faces a million times. Wide mouths, wild eyes, and flailing limbs, every one of them looked as if they ran on the edge of their balance. Tilting forward as they moved in their desire to get at their prey, they still somehow moved with the pace of athletes—even the fat ones.

The ropes were just a few metres away, so Vicky focused solely on them, her legs damp with dew, her pulse pounding through her skull. They hung above a sharp hill that ran about three metres down and was steep enough to resemble a small cliff.

When Vicky reached the edge of it and jumped, she caught the rope with both hands and clamped the large knot at the bottom with both of her feet. As the rope swung, she scrabbled up it, her palms clammy with sweat.

The higher Vicky moved, the less effect the rope's pendulous swing had on her. It travelled back and forth as she shimmied a couple of metres up to another knot. She held herself there and watched Serj leap for his rope.

A few seconds later, Serj—breathing so heavily he looked like he'd vomit—climbed up as high as Vicky.

The herd of diseased ran for the pair. The lead one—a large black man so bald the sun bounced off his shiny head and created a sharp glare—reached out for Vicky's rope as the ground disappeared beneath him. Although he batted the knot at the bottom, he didn't have the co-ordination to grip on and his legs folded as he fell down the steep hill.

The rest of the pack followed him over. They moved like a herd of spooked animals driven over the edge of a cliff. All of them made a pathetic attempt to grab the ropes that Vicky and Serj held onto. All of them missed.

Vicky watched them stack up on the ground below. They turned into a rotten pile of entangled limbs. Every time one tried to get to its feet, another one fell over the top and knocked it down again. Cracks, slaps, and screams came up at them as the bodies collided. She winced as heads smashed against cheeks and knees cracked temples.

***

Once all of the diseased had fallen over the edge, Vicky looked back the way they'd come from. A fresh breeze ran across the field they'd just crossed, swaying the long grass. The dew glittered in the bright morning sun. She looked all the way to the woods they'd run through, the grass pressed down along the path they'd taken so many times before. There didn't seem to be any more diseased.

When Vicky looked at Serj, Serj nodded.

After a deep breath, Vicky climbed higher up the rope. The coarseness of it burned her palms and exhaustion turned her arms weak. No matter how fit she got, the run always wore her out; fear had a way of taking its pound of flesh.

Most of the diseased below them had gotten to their feet; when Vicky looked down, she saw a sea of twisted, cut, and bloody faces. The run through the trees and the collisions with one another seemed to have taken its toll on them. They stared up at her through their red and crusty eyes, and they bit at the air like they could taste her.

At the top of her rope, Vicky grabbed a second, skinnier rope. Two gates sat below her. The thinner cord in her hand ran to the first gate directly at the bottom of the hill. It stood between the diseased and their route back out of there. When she gave it a sharp tug, it removed the block holding the gate in place. Gravity helped the gate fall forward, gathering momentum until it slammed shut with a loud *crash* and penned the diseased in.

Vicky raised her eyebrows at Serj. "No matter how many times we do this, I can't relax until now."

So used to the reek of the diseased, Vicky only smelled them now she'd calmed down a little. The heady stink of rot rose at her as if it curdled the air. She looked out over the pen at all of the other diseased they'd caught. About two hundred of them in total, they made their way over to the newest arrivals, their blank and bloody eyes looking up at Vicky and Serj.

"I hate the way those fuckers *stare* at us," Serj said.

Vicky's stomach sank to take in the emaciated ex-humans, the sight of them no less potent despite living with them for years. "It's amazing, isn't it? They've been in this world for over a decade and they're still consumed with their desire to get to us."

"And it's no less horrifying to look at," Serj added.

Vicky reached out and pulled on another rope. It ran to the catch on a second gate, which separated the new arrivals from the main pen. When she pulled it, the second gate swung open and gave the new diseased access to the rest of their enclosure. It also let the other diseased out into the containment area, but with the outer gate now closed, they couldn't get any farther than that.

After Vicky had shimmied down to the knot at the bottom of her rope, she looked at Serj again. "You ready for this?"

Several shades paler than his usual Indian hue, Serj gulped, his Adam's apple lifting and dropping again. "I *hate* this bit."

"You've done it countless times before and been fine *every* time."

"I still worry I could misjudge it and end up down *there* with *them*."

"If you do," Vicky said, swinging back and forth on the rope like a playful child, "I'll still remember to say good morning to your diseased arse when I come and visit."

"Gee, thanks!" Serj said.

When Vicky had enough motion, she focused on the patch of high ground they'd come from and let go of the rope.

The moment of weightlessness made Vicky's stomach turn backflips and her arms flailed as she flew through the air. A sharp jolt snapped through her when she hit the hard ground, solid for the lack of rain that summer. When she turned around, she saw Serj launch himself after her.

Maybe she hadn't managed it any better than Serj, but to see him fly through the air—his arms and legs wild, his mouth wide in a silent scream—made her smile.

A *thud* and Serj hit the ground, his legs giving way beneath him.

Vicky held her hand out and smiled at him. "You okay?"

Another gulp and Serj gasped. "Yep. Although I still stand by what I said."

"Which is?"

"You're *insane*."

Vicky laughed. "I was like that as a kid, you know? Whenever I got the chance to do something nuts, I would. I'd swan dive from the sofa, try somersaults I couldn't land on the patio in the back garden, throw stones at windows. Although, I'd like to think I consider the consequences more now."

Vicky walked back toward the steep slope they'd led the diseased over and stared at the penned-in crowd. She smiled. "But look at what we have now."

The sound of two hundred or more diseased groaning and

shuffling called through the otherwise still morning air.

When Serj walked up next to her and looked at the sea of infection down below, he shook his head. "Yeah, just look at them. What an *achievement*! It looks like a scene from Dante's *Inferno*."

"Don't be so soft, Serj."

Serj didn't reply; instead, he backed away and Vicky followed him. They still had more to do.

***

It might have been early enough for the sun to still be low in the sky and for the ground to be covered in dew, but being June and cloudless, the day rapidly heated up and sweat itched beneath Vicky's collar. A thirst bit into her throat that swallowing couldn't sate; it tasted like dust. She couldn't see the pen of diseased from her current position. They'd backed far enough away and the sudden drop in the landscape hid it from view, but she could still hear their groaning discontent and smell their rotten stench. It smelled so rich they could have been lying next to her.

They knew what to do—they'd done it plenty of times before—so without a word, Vicky nodded at Serj and he ran off to their left. A wide arc around the side of the pen meant he could approach it without being seen.

***

The sound of the diseased had died down. They'd clearly forgotten about the humans they'd seen in the tree, so when a cacophony of screaming fury exploded to life again, Vicky took that as her cue.

Vicky walked close to the sharp drop and peered down at the pen. She did her best to remain hidden. It wouldn't be the end of the world if they noticed her, but it would drag the process out even longer. At that thought, her stomach rumbled. She needed to get back to Home for some breakfast.

Fortunately, their plan worked well that morning. All of the diseased focused their attention on Serj when he appeared at the other side of the pen by the river. He waved his arms and jumped on the spot. Vicky couldn't help but smile at the sight of him. With the newly trapped diseased joining the others in the corner by Serj, she slowly slid down the hill to the first gate.

While holding her breath and with her heart beating in her chest, Vicky pulled the gate open towards her. The hinges creaked, but the diseased seemed too occupied with Serj to notice.

Vicky slipped through the opening and eased the gate closed behind her to stop it from slamming shut. That had happened once before; a loud crash, and the diseased had turned on her as one savage force. They'd sprinted for the second, open gate, making it a race between them and her. She'd won that day, pulling the second gate closed and penning them in. But it had been close.

In the same way the first gate had slammed shut into its latch when Vicky had pulled on the rope, the second gate had swung open away from its latch. It meant she had to close it now so they could reset the trap.

The pack of diseased shuffled and screamed as they focused their attention on Serj. It didn't matter how many times Vicky stood between the two gates, in her current position—exposed until she locked the second one—panic always threatened to reach up and choke her.

Vicky drew a deep breath, ran into the pen for the second gate, grabbed the middle of it, and dragged it backwards with her. By the time the diseased had turned in response to the sharp groan of the old hinges, she'd already beaten them. A loud *crash* and the gate slammed shut.

The diseased rushed over and slammed into the locked gate as if they hadn't seen it. Vicky watched them as she backed away and placed the block back beneath the first gate, propping it open for their next entrapment.

She then climbed the hill, her back to the monsters in the pen, her legs aching from the short yet steep ascent. The gate did enough to contain the diseased. The second the stupid bastards realised just how practical their opposable thumbs were, they'd be fucked. Until then, the dumb monsters could be easily contained.

At the top of the hill, Vicky looked across the pen and gave Serj a thumbs-up. Serj returned the gesture before he turned around and headed in the direction of Home.

***

On their way back to Home, Serj shook his head. "You're fucking insane."

The sounds of the trapped diseased came from behind them and rode the air. But they wouldn't be able to hear them from Home, so they didn't have to tell the others—not yet anyway. "Yep," Vicky said, "but it'll work. Trust me."

Chapter Two

As Vicky walked along the corridor with Flynn beside her, she inhaled the acerbic bite of bleach in the air and looked down. The floor had dents, dirty scratches, and stains, but she couldn't see a single tear or rip in the blue linoleum. It had held up to over a decade's worth of use. Other than the sound of her and Flynn's footsteps, she heard little else.

A barbed lump lodged in Vicky's throat as she marched on. Flynn hadn't taken well to the idea, but—like she'd told him—they needed to do it to move forward. The threat of tears itched her eyeballs, but she held them back. She could hardly cry considering she was the one who insisted this needed to happen.

When they drew closer to the kitchen, the whir of its large extractor fan called down the corridor at them. Boiled cabbage pushed the smell of bleach away. No matter what time of day, the kitchen always smelled the same. A loud crash sounded out and Vicky jumped; someone had just dropped a metal pan while making breakfast.

Vicky didn't have much to do with the kitchen staff. They always seemed too busy to talk, so she didn't bother. Let Serj deal with them if they needed to communicate at all.

When they reached the end of the corridor and stepped into the large space containing the kitchen, Vicky looked over at the staff and none of them looked back. Apparently they were like that with everyone—everyone except Jessica. She didn't need to think about her at that moment, not with her emotions already on the surface.

Vicky walked through the huge hall, heading for the corridor near the medical bay. Flynn remained beside her, matching her step for step and still not speaking.

When they got closer, the metallic tang of Jessica's spilled blood returned to Vicky's sense memory. She looked at the shitty bed they'd put her on and shook her head. They'd been woefully ill-equipped to deal with anything other than a blister, and even then they would have struggled. Jessica hadn't stood a fucking chance.

When Vicky looked at Flynn—his bottom lip pushed out in a slight frown—she saw that he too stared at the medic bay. No doubt he had similar thoughts as her own.

Once they reached the corridor running parallel to the one Vicky stayed in, they cut into it and headed toward Flynn's new room.

Vicky walked into the room first and Flynn followed her, carrying his bedding from where he'd brought it from their shared room.

Like the corridors, the room stank of bleach. It also had the same white walls and blue floor. She'd got so used to two beds, it looked sparse with just a single bed and a bedside table.

A cough to clear her throat—which did little for the lump

still in it—and Vicky said, "So this is your new room." She couldn't hide the warble in her voice.

Although Flynn stared at her—a heavy scowl darkening his features—he didn't reply.

"Come on, mate, you knew this day had to happen. You hate how overbearing I am. I know you're only sixteen, but I think you're old enough to sleep in your own room. If you stay too close to me, I'll carry on being that annoying mum that wants to do *everything* for you." Vicky smiled as she looked up into his brown eyes and round face. "When I look at you, I still see the little boy we rescued from a tree. You were the only survivor that day, you know?"

Flynn continued to stare at her without response.

"It's true. None of us have spoken much about it because it was such a harrowing time. Your dad and I arrived at your school and the place had been ripped to shreds. There were bodies of little kids and teachers everywhere. There seemed no way you could have survived. Then your dad thought about the tree and how much you loved to climb. Good job we checked that, eh?"

Vicky stepped closer to Flynn and hugged his huge frame. When he hugged her back, he damn near squeezed the life from her. "You understand, don't you?" she whispered to him.

She felt him nod, but he didn't speak.

"And don't tell me you're not getting pissed off with me keeping on doing things for you. I need to let you grow up and be the young man you're ready to be. Otherwise, we'll just keep on arguing about me getting in the way.

"Besides, you'll have Piotr with you. Now we've swapped the dead soil in the farms with fertile stuff from outside, Piotr can leave the farm and become a guard. He'll be a great mentor to you."

After Vicky stepped back a pace, she held her hands out to Flynn. She gave his strong grip a squeeze and he squeezed back. A damp film covered his large brown eyes, but he didn't cry. She didn't cry either, as hard as she found it not to.

"We'll still do a lot of stuff together. As guards, we'll need to work as a team when we go on missions outside."

Silence.

"I'm going back to my room now, okay?" Vicky said.

Flynn nodded and lifted his chin. The sad look had left his eyes to be replaced with a detached steely glaze.

Vicky turned around and walked out of the room. By the time she'd got three steps from him into the corridor, she blinked a single tear. The track of it turned cold against her cheek.

Chapter Three

Vicky made sure she closed the door behind her and Serj. They needed to keep the muggy heat in. The humid atmosphere clung to her skin like a film coating, and the air stank of damp soil. When she gulped, she tasted mud on the back of her throat.

Rufus, the new head of the farm, looked up at them.

"So everything's going okay since we swapped the soil round?" Vicky asked.

A hippy in a previous life, Rufus seemed permanently in awe of nature. His face lit up, his eyes going from half shut to wide open as he sprang to life. "Things have been *awesome*. I know supplies are low at the moment, but give it a few months and I'm sure we'll be back to full capacity." The tall and slender man pulled his long hair away from his face and smiled. "Maybe sooner."

Piotr had already given them that information before he'd joined the guards, but Vicky and Serj liked to check in case Rufus needed anything. Whatever happened, they couldn't afford for the food to run out.

The heat pressed so forcefully against her skin, Vicky twisted and writhed almost as if she could worm her way free of it. She looked at Serj. "Right, can we go now?"

Serj nodded and opened the door back out into the corridor.

Not cold in the corridor, but the change in temperature cooled Vicky's sweat-dampened skin as she walked along with Serj beside her.

Serj held his bottom lip in a pinch, frowned, and stared straight ahead. "I keep worrying the crops will fail again."

"Me too. Rufus seems to have a handle on things though. We can catch any problems as they occur as long as we keep checking in on them."

Although Serj nodded at Vicky's comment, he didn't reply.

As straight as an arrow flies, the corridor led all the way to the kitchen in the centre of Home. Over one hundred metres away, Vicky could see the occasional chef's-whites-covered arm or leg as they worked at preparing the food. She could even see through the kitchen to the corridor beyond, the one with her bedroom on it. If she squinted, she could see movement in the canteen at the end of that too.

When they passed the room Hugh had planted Jessica's body in, Vicky looked at Serj and reached across to put a comforting hand on his back.

Serj shrugged it off.

Vicky listened to the sound of someone running on a treadmill in the gym in one of the rooms farther along. She inhaled the bleach in the air. As a child, she'd lived in the countryside, and every year the smell of muck spreading made her feel at home. The aroma of bleach had a similar effect now. To smell it meant safety. Certainty in an uncertain world.

"I think we should open that room up again," Serj said.

A look at the locked door and Vicky frowned at him. "So soon?"

"It's not too soon for me."

The tone suggested it was, but Vicky didn't point that out. Instead, she said, "It may be too soon for the community though. It's still pretty raw for most people."

Serj shot a blast of air from between pursed lips. "Well, they need to get over it, then. We can't keep it locked *forever*."

"Actually, with the amount of spare rooms we have in this place, we probably can."

The conversation between them died again for a second.

"Look," Vicky said, "just let me know when you want it opened up and I'll make sure it happens, yeah?"

"I don't care," Serj replied. "Do it whenever you like."

Vicky let it drop as they drew closer to the gym. The table they'd set up for Flynn remained outside the room. Although instead of Flynn manning it, they'd given the job to someone a little younger. Alf—twelve years old and so tall he had to duck to enter most rooms—seemed pleased when they offered him the position. The boy already towered over her and he probably had more growing in him. He even stood a few inches taller than Piotr, who topped out at at least six feet four inches. The boy had a curtain-style haircut that hung in his eyes.

Before they got to him, Alf looked at the stopwatch around his neck and stood up. An origami child, he unfolded himself from his seat, his long limbs like spaghetti as he moved to the gym's entrance. A queue of about seven people lined up waiting their turn. "Excuse me, sir," Alf called into the room. Vicky couldn't tell who he spoke to from her current position.

"*Excuse* me," the boy said again.

With a voice higher than it should have been for someone his size, Alf spoke again. "*Sir*, you need to move on now. Your time's up and we have quite a few people waiting."

An average-sized man in every way—about five feet nine inches, a paunch, and white hair—walked from the gym and passed the boy on his way through. He shot Alf a glare and then moved past the line of people with his attention on the ground.

Just as the person at the front of the queue—a short black woman who Vicky didn't know by name—stepped forward, a man behind her shoved past.

Alf restrained him by pushing a large palm into his chest.

The man clenched his jaw as he looked up at the boy.

"I'm sorry, sir," Alf said, "but you need to wait your turn. This lady's been here longer than you, so she's next."

"But I've been waiting *hours*."

"Join the queue," Alf replied. Then before the man could respond, he added, "Oh, you already have, and you're *second* in it."

"Don't get smart with me, *boy*."

Before it could go any further, Serj cleared his throat. The man and Alf turned to look at him. "Everything okay?"

A look at one another and Alf nodded while he kept his focus on the pushy man. "Everything's fine." He stepped aside to let the short black lady in and Vicky held her smile back. It made her happy to see the younger generation being given more responsibility. They all needed to grow up eventually.

A flushed face and the man refused to make eye contact with

either Serj or Vicky as he returned to the queue. They both let it slide as they waited for Alf to fold back into his seat before they spoke to him.

"Everything's going well, then?" Serj asked.

The boy nodded and grinned, clearly still stoked about his appointment. "Yep."

"Good, you're doing a grand job."

"Thanks, the queues have been crazy for weeks now. Everyone's trying to get fit for the impending war."

An anxious bristle shimmered down the line at the mention of the future conflict. It also seemed to give the tired and slouched queue a little boost, as many of them straightened their backs and nodded in agreement with Alf's statement.

"That's sensible," Vicky said while watching them all, "because it won't be long now. It won't be long at all."

Chapter Four

The guy might have been twice Vicky's size, but that much weight—running at her like a stampeding rhino—became easy to manipulate when she grabbed his swinging arm and flung him over her shoulder.

Jackson hit the blue mat hard and it drove the air from his body with a loud *oomph*.

Red-faced from the exertion, and probably shame, the large man stared up at Vicky and fought to get his breath under control.

"Now that," Vicky said as she paced the blue, padded mat in front of the gathered residents, "is how you use someone else's momentum against them."

She held her hand down to Jackson and helped him get to his feet. She bowed at the man and he bowed back before he joined the others along the far wall.

"I've never trained in a martial art," Vicky said as she continued to pace the mat, the plastic surface cold against her bare feet, "but I have fought the diseased for over a decade now. It's made me calm in tense situations and able to telegraph people's movements. I'm not saying you all need that, but sparring is important. To try to outsmart your partner will teach you the valuable skills needed in combat. If you've dodged a blow a thousand times in training, the theory is you'll dodge it when the pressure's on." The sound of her voice carried through the amphitheater of the canteen.

When Vicky first started training the people of Home, they would move the tables and chairs to one side of the space, lay the blue mats down, and put everything away afterwards. As the residents got used to the slightly more cramped eating conditions, they left the mats out. Now half of the canteen had been allocated to gym work permanently, and at any one time there would always be someone training in it.

Also, moving the tables closer together had helped the community bond. Where they had once eaten on opposite sides of the canteen, they now ate side by side and socialised more. They'd grown into a tight team. A team that would hopefully be ready to go out and fight Moira's community soon.

"I'm pleased to see how you've all progressed," Vicky said as she continued to pace. Although Serj had been appointed the leader of Home, she took the responsibility for combat and the outside world. She knew it better than him.

"We need to be ready to go to war any day now, and all of you are much fitter, leaner versions of your previous selves. For that, you should be proud."

A glance over at the tables in the other half of the canteen and Vicky saw the remains of breakfast. Most mornings they did breakfast from seven till nine, but on a Tuesday, when Vicky had her meetings, they did it from six thirty till eight. Everyone had to be done by eight and ready. She didn't normally adopt an authoritarian approach, but the discipline seemed to help the residents get in the zone. As a result, breakfast never got cleared away on a Tuesday until after training. "We have a new guard I'd like to introduce you all to."

With a beckoning hand, Vicky encouraged the lady to step forward. "This is Scoop," Vicky said. "Most of you know her, but for those who don't, just take her in for a moment."

A lean and toned woman of Jamaican descent, Scoop had dreadlocks down to her arse and a scowl that could level cities. Despite knowing most of them, she looked at the gathered people like she'd fight anyone who wanted it. Although in truth, she had a heart of gold. Once she let you in, she never let go, and now she'd joined the guards, Home would be a safer place.

"Scoop's daughter, Meisha, is fourteen now and old enough to take better care of herself," Vicky said. "It's given Scoop more time. Where she's always wanted to help out, she now can."

Vicky watched Scoop's hard scowl lift when she looked at her daughter. The heavy set spread into a broad smile and then dropped again as quickly as it had appeared when she continued to look down the line.

"Now before we get to training, I want to spar with someone else." A look up and down at the gathered residents and Vicky put her hands on her hips. "I need a volunteer. Who wants to test their skills?"

A man named William stepped forward. At over six feet tall, he stood a good eight inches above Vicky. Wide-shouldered and with thick biceps, he nodded at her. "Are you *sure* you want me to go for you?"

"You can try."

The man laughed, as did a few other men in the crowd. They never seemed to learn, their male ego always telling them they had the beating of a woman.

"I needed to check," he said.

"No, you didn't." Vicky widened her stance and stared at William. About thirty metres of blue crash mat separated them, so she beckoned him forward. Like the last man, William charged at her.

"Moira's community haven't attacked yet," Vicky said as she felt the vibration of William's heavy footfalls rush towards her through the mats, "but they will."

Just a few metres separated them and William wound back, his punch coming from a mile off. When he swung, Vicky dropped to the ground and rolled away from him.

Several steps past her, William spun around and scowled.

"Does anyone have any questions about what we're going to face soon?"

William came at Vicky again. She had most of her attention on the man, but she still noticed the raised hand from one of the residents. Even if she hadn't, the collective groan said it all.

A much better attempt at masking his attack, Vicky still saw William's fake lunge and jumped to the side to avoid the real punch from his left hand. Before he'd passed her, she dropped down and swiped his legs away. A second later, the ground shook when he hit it.

"Ignore them, Stuart," Vicky said to the slightly podgy man with the raised hand.

Stuart nodded and asked one of the many questions he'd no

doubt ask that day. "How many people are there in Moira's community?"

When Vicky had worked in an office, she'd hated meetings the most. They'd always moved at a glacial pace, as everyone had to stay with the tempo of the stupidest person in the room. It had been even more galling when the thickest person there had been her boss. However, now she had to lead the meetings, she had a fresh perspective on it. Sure, Stuart didn't have it going on upstairs, but he had something to offer. Simply being willing and able would make him an asset on the battlefield. She couldn't treat him like everyone else did because he'd be by her side when she needed it most. "I still don't know that," she said.

"You don't even have a rough idea?"

"No."

William came at Vicky from behind. At the last minute, she dodged to the right. The haymaker swooshed through the air above Vicky's head.

As if to teach him a lesson, Vicky jumped back up and kicked him up the arse on his way through.

"How many prisoners, then?" Stuart asked.

"Jesus, Stuart," one of the other men—maybe Ben, but Vicky couldn't remember his name—said. "How many times do you want to ask the *same* bloody questions? What do you want Vicky to say to you?"

"I ... I don't know. I just thought she might have gone past the community on her travels and have more information. I'd like to know what we're going into."

"Hell," Ben said. "We're going into hell."

Vicky stepped in to diffuse the situation. "I'd imagine she

has about twenty still, Stuart. I haven't been back since they trapped me, but from what I saw, the number of prisoners changes all the time. She kills some, she finds some more, she kills some …"

Another rhino charge came from over Vicky's right shoulder, which she avoided. As William shot past her, she said, "You need to get lighter on your feet. You ain't sneaking up on anything if you move like that." It didn't help that he stank of sweat too, but she kept that to herself.

Shame, anger, tiredness … whatever had set fire to William's cheeks looked like it had taken root. A fury burned in his eyes.

"You can go back against the wall now, William. And remember to work on your movement. I've no doubt you hit like a steam train, you just need to make sure you can move with enough stealth to land one of your punches."

As William found his place against the wall, Vicky looked over at Flynn and pulled a tight smile. The boy returned the same tense gesture. They'd not spoken since she'd moved him to his new room two days ago.

The children lined up at the end, as they had done since Vicky started her meetings. She walked over to them and smiled at their chubby faces as she continued to address the room. "It's been working well to take the children outside of Home. I think it's important they understand what we're up against from a young age. Who knows when they'll need to fight. If they're ready for it now, then hopefully it'll save lives. Although I don't think we should take them any farther than the solar panels at the moment." If any of the residents ventured too far, they might find the pen of diseased. That would be a hard one to explain to the group. They hadn't even told the other guards about it yet.

When Vicky got near the corner of the room, she looked at the collection of spears resting there. The tip of each one—made from different types of scavenged metal—caught the light. The world had an abundance of cutlery, tin cans, and scraps of cars, so they'd taken everything they could find, sharpened them into points, and attached them to long, straight sticks. She picked up a particularly large one and looked down its length like she would a snooker cue. "This collection is coming along nicely. These spears could be the difference between life and death, so keep making them."

After she'd replaced the spear, Vicky looked along the line at the people. "Before we start training for the day, does anyone have any questions?"

Everyone turned to look at Stuart. His pale face turned crimson and he shook his head.

"Good," Vicky said. "Serj and I will go to the local town later on today. We need to get a few supplies. We're not taking requests, I'm afraid; we won't be able to carry it all."

The glare from Flynn tugged on Vicky's attention and she turned to look at the boy. He seemed pissed, like he expected to go out with them too.

"Although we won't be here, Scoop, Piotr, and Flynn will, and they'll be able to help anyone who needs it."

Vicky clapped her hands together and the sound carried through the open space. "Right, well done, everyone. Keep up the good work and we'll keep you informed of when we plan to attack Moira's community."

Vicky then left the canteen and headed for her room. Covered in the sweat of the two guys she'd sparred with, she needed to shower and get some clean clothes on.

Chapter Five

"It's hard to believe this used to be a road," Vicky said to Serj as they walked, the long grass up to her waist. "Were it not for all these cars, it'd be impossible to tell."

Sweat glistened on Serj's brow and he breathed heavily from their fast pace. "What I'd give to be able to drive a car into town now," he said.

The ruins of what used to be the local town stood on the horizon. Vicky squinted against the bright sun as she focused on the tall glassless tower that dominated the skyline. "I like to think of the days when cars queued on this road to get in and out of town," she said.

Serj's dark hair danced in the strong wind and he squinted from where it lashed against his eyes. "You *like* to think of traffic jams?"

"Life was simpler then, you know? We had our worries, sure, and maybe it didn't feel simpler at the time, but hindsight being a wonderful thing and all that …"

Shrugging, Serj pulled a tight-lipped smile.

Vicky rolled her shoulders to help her crossbow sit more

comfortably on her back. She reached down to touch the knife strapped to her belt. Paranoid she wouldn't be able to grab it in an emergency, she'd already touched the handle for reassurance about fifty times in the past twenty minutes.

"Do you ever worry about upsetting the people in Home?" Serj asked.

It felt good to stretch her legs, and Vicky drew a deep breath of the fresh outside air before she responded. "What do you mean?"

"Well, you know …" Serj cleared his throat.

"No. What?"

"You're quite … direct. You don't take any shit, which I admire, but don't you worry it's not good for morale?"

"Fuck morale."

Serj flinched at the comment and then smiled. "See what I mean?"

Vicky laughed. "Okay, maybe not fuck morale, but I'm more concerned about getting the people of Home ready to fight. If they resent me for it and survive, then so be it. If I go too easy on them, they'll die. And more importantly, the people I love will die."

"Flynn, you mean?"

"Of course. I'll do anything to protect him. So if I need to ruffle a few feathers now to save lives in the future, then so be it. I'm not here to make friends. At least, not until Moira's community has fallen." Vicky checked her knife again.

"But you still have to live with them."

The conversation faded away and Vicky listened to the sounds of nature around them. The caw of a crow, the swooshing of the long grass, the scuff of their boots as they walked over the hard road surface. They might not have been able to see it, and it had plenty of cracks running through it, but after being chased through uneven fields by the diseased, the ground definitely felt like a road.

***

As they entered the town, Vicky looked up at the large round-fronted office block she'd seen from miles away. It looked as she remembered it … a framework of steel, smashed windows, abandoned desks, chairs, wastepaper baskets. A yellowed sheet of newspaper skittered across the road in front of them as they walked beneath an old railway bridge. For some reason the grass hadn't pushed through the road as successfully here. Tufts sprouted through cracks, but on the whole, the roads remained usable. Not that she'd seen any working vehicles in a long time.

To look up at the top of the building from the ground hurt the back of Vicky's neck and made her dizzy. Desperation had driven her to hang from such a high spot when her and Hugh had been chased up there; nothing else would have brought that out in her.

Several broken bodies lay on the ground in front of them. All of them had the look of twisted horror synonymous with the diseased. Rigor mortis had frozen their pained expressions as they cured in the sunshine.

A look across at Serj and Vicky saw him taking the scene in. "It was here when I realised something was up with him."

"Who?" Serj said as he continued to study the bodies of the fallen.

"Hugh."

When Serj pulled his axe from the harness on his back, Vicky did the same with her crossbow and checked she could reach her knife on her hip by touching the handle.

"What is it?" Vicky asked Serj, her eyes stinging from refusing to blink as she scanned their surroundings.

"Nothing. I just want to be ready."

Vicky eased her stance a little but kept her crossbow drawn.

"With this building in the way," Serj said as he pointed at the large office block, "it's much harder to see if anything's coming. Better to be prepared, eh?"

Vicky nodded. "We got chased into that building," she said. "A herd picked up our tail and we had nowhere else to go. We ended up on the top floor with a pack of them behind us." She pointed at the diseased on the ground. "We managed to avoid some of them, but Hugh shit himself. He couldn't keep it together and properly panicked. If he'd had any military training, he would have been able to cope with the pressure."

"He lost his head?"

"And then some. The guy went to *pieces*. Door kicking in Mogadishu … what a fucking clown! How he got this far in this world, I don't know."

"He had the keys to Home." Clearly aggravated by the wind, which played havoc with Vicky's hair too, Serj pulled his fringe from his eyes again and held it there as he looked at her, his axe still raised.

"Yeah, I think you're right. He gave it the big 'I am' behind a locked door, but I don't think he would have survived any other way."

"I don't think many of us would."

And he had a point. Vicky had probably been an exceptional case by surviving for years when so many would have fallen. They'd been lucky to find a shelter like Home. Had Vicky found it too, maybe she would be much softer for it.

"I knew all along, you know?" Serj said.

Vicky looked at him, his dark eyes pinching from where he winced against the elements. "Huh?"

"About him and Jessica." Serj spoke through clenched teeth. "I *knew* the filthy slut was fucking him. *Everyone* did. They treated me like a mug." The Adam's apple on his neck bobbed from gulping and his words wavered. "I'm glad they're both gone. Fuck them. It's a fresh start for me now and I'm not going to let *anyone* treat me like that again."

Although Vicky opened her mouth to respond, she didn't get the words out. The scream—somewhere between a shriek and a roar—came into the town from the fields behind them. Serj's eyes widened as her heart kicked.

"Fuck!" Serj said and spun in the direction of the noise.

"Whatever happens"—Vicky looked back underneath the railway bridge and saw nothing—"I ain't going back in that building."

She didn't need a response and Serj didn't give her one. Instead, he ran down the road that forked around the left side of the building and Vicky followed.

The diseased were too far away to have seen them, but maybe they'd picked up on their scent. Whatever drove the mob forward, Vicky and Serj needed to get out of there.

They passed an old gallery, art in the windows that probably had some worth in the old world, then an old fried chicken shop; the image of a bearded man that looked like Santa remained intact even if a little bleached by the sun. They passed a pub on their left and Serj ducked down an alleyway next to it.

The call of the diseased followed them. The blood-curdling sound turned Vicky's tired legs weak as she ran on Serj's heels. Two steps into the alley, her stomach sank. What the fuck had they just run into?

Serj disappeared around to the right at the end of the alley.

Before Vicky got there, she heard him say, "Fuck!"

When Vicky rounded the corner, she looked up at the tall wall. It stood easily ten metres high. She fought for breath, the confined space giving an echo to her heavy respiration. "Fuck!"

Serj moved back and forth in the enclosed space like a demented dog. He shook his head. "I'm sorry, Vicky. I'm *so* sorry. I've fucked up big time."

And he had, but what could she say? It would serve no purpose to have a go at him now.

As the sounds of the diseased drew closer, Vicky inhaled a deep breath and raised her crossbow. She'd only jump out and use it when she had to. If she could reload quickly enough, maybe she'd take out a few before they got close. She touched the handle of her knife.

The crossbow shook in Vicky's grip, but she kept the stock against her shoulder, closed one eye, and looked down the barrel, ready to jump out.

The stampede closed in on the alley. The group screamed and Vicky saw Serj jump in her peripheral vision. She spoke to him in a whisper while still looking down her crossbow. "They haven't seen us yet, we'll be *fine*."

The second she finished her assertion, the clumsy footsteps of what sounded like a solitary diseased entered the alleyway. Fortunately, the sound of the others thundered straight past. She looked at Serj, who raised his axe.

A nasally, rattled, and rasping breath moved closer to them, but they remained out of its line of sight. The thing sounded like a bulldog with respiratory problems. Its gasps spoke of how far it had run to get to the town. But the rest hadn't homed in on Vicky and Serj, so what the fuck were they hunting?

By the time the beast had made it about halfway down the alley, Vicky's breathing had leveled out. One bolt could end it. But could she get it off before the thing screamed? If the sound of footsteps had been anything to go by, the swarm of diseased in the town would end them within seconds. Whatever happened, the solitary fucker in the alley couldn't be allowed to give them away.

Vicky scraped her left shoulder against the brick wall as she leaned into it, watching the bend in the alley for the thing to appear.

The clumsy steps drew closer.

When the thing's shadow preceded it, spreading across the ground as a dark oil spill, Vicky smelled the funk of rot. She swallowed a dry gulp, stale from the air being polluted by its presence, and waited for the diseased's face so she could fire a bolt into it. One final inhale to steady her rampaging heart and she put a gentle squeeze on the bow's trigger.

Chapter Six

The diseased's breaths sounded like an old motorbike engine, stuttering and inconsistent as it shuffled closer to Vicky. She glanced at Serj once more, who continued to hold his axe aloft. The diseased had drawn so close now the cloying stench of rot damn near choked her. She clenched her jaw against its invasive probe and readied herself to release a bolt into its face.

Vicky closed her left eye and continued to look down the barrel of her crossbow at the space she expected the thing to appear in.

A loud scream shot through the city. A human scream, the sound of fear from a non-diseased. It flew through the streets and Vicky jumped. It took all her restraint to stop from pulling the crossbow's trigger, her finger tensing on the small piece of metal.

The beast—just centimetres from seeing them—screamed in response to the sound, its shrill call bouncing off the tight alley's walls before it sprinted away. As the heavy footsteps retreated up the alleyway, Vicky let go of the tension in her upper body and lowered her weapon. But she couldn't yet take her eyes from the space she'd expected it to appear in. She reached down to touch her knife strapped to her hip and watched just in case.

After a few minutes, Vicky let go of a hard exhale and looked across at Serj. Paler than she'd ever seen him, he breathed quickly. "That was close!"

"You're telling me," she said. "I feel sorry for the poor bastard who just screamed."

Serj nodded.

Vicky sighed.

***

A couple of minutes passed, during which time Vicky listened to the sound of the diseased in the town fade. Although she could still hear something. Maybe her imagination, it sounded like they hadn't completely left the area. Probably just her imagination.

Vicky checked her knife at her hip again, raised her crossbow, and led the way back up the alley. She paused after every step. They'd heard the diseased run away, but you could never be too careful in this new chaotic world. And if any of them found her and Serj in the alley, they'd be fucked. No room to fight and nowhere to run to. The thought quickened her pulse.

After her next step, Vicky screwed her nose up at the ammonia reek of urine. She looked at Serj; with his own nose ruffled, he seemed to also notice the smell. "It's been a decade since people went out on the piss on the weekend and this alley still stinks of urine."

Serj shook his head. "Maybe it's animals?"

"I hope so, we could do with finding something to eat."

At the end of the alley, Vicky peered out and looked up and down what seemed to be an abandoned road. She pulled her head back in. "Looks clear."

That seemed to be good enough for Serj, who suddenly strode past Vicky out into the street. What a time to find his confidence! He led the way toward the old high street and Vicky followed.

After a couple of steps, Serj broke into a jog and Vicky sped up to keep pace with him. She scanned their surroundings as she ran, peering into darkened buildings in case any diseased lay in wait.

Once Serj reached a large abandoned shop, he slowed down. The kind of place that sold everything, the white writing on the sign above the door still displayed the shop's name.

"Wilkinson's," Vicky said, "I remember these places. When Woolworths went out of business, this lot sprang up everywhere. I wouldn't mind betting all the hammers, axes, saws—in fact, anything of any use—are gone."

Serj shrugged. "Probably."

Glass dust covered the pavement outside the shop like glitter and sparkled in the strong sun.

Serj walked toward the place and Vicky followed him. They stepped through the bent chrome frames of the front doors where a large sheet of glass had once been. Very few windows remained after ten chaotic years.

Clearly less trodden than the pavement outside, the glass inside the shop still had some bite left and it crunched beneath Vicky's steps, as popping candy would. She stopped, checked her knife, and looked back outside the shop one last time. Now that she'd moved slightly farther forward, she saw what had once been a McDonald's across the way. A vast building on the corner, it had two floors. Like every other property in the area, it had no windows left. It made it easier to hear the diseased when they screamed from inside the place.

Serj walked next to Vicky and she blocked any further progress with an arm across his chest. "Whatever's happening over there," she said in a whisper, "we need to make sure we're gone before it becomes our problem. The diseased will get bored, or they'll feed. Either way, they won't stay in there forever."

Serj squinted as he looked across the way. "But what are they chasing? Maybe there's someone in there that needs our help."

"And you think we can help them?"

After a few more seconds of peering out of the shop, Serj shrugged and looked down at the ground. "No, I suppose not."

Dark from the lights no longer working, the store had been turned over, as Vicky had expected it to be. She checked the knife on her hip as she looked around the place. Shelving units had been toppled, some of the larger ones leaning up against the others like dominos yet to fall flat. They looked like they could crash down at any moment.

Black tyre tracks marked the mauve floor from where motorbikes had been ridden through the place. It must have happened years ago, but Vicky still tensed at the sight of them and checked her knife again.

As they padded through the shop, Vicky listened to the screams of the diseased outside. It fought for her attention, but she kept her focus on Serj and their surroundings. The diseased wouldn't know about them if they kept a low profile.

"You seem to know your way around," Vicky said as she followed Serj's quick pace.

"I came out scavenging a few years back. We always had most of what we needed in Home, so I didn't do it often. But I came out a few times. Once with Jessica. We weren't together then and I was trying to impress her. I wanted to show her just how brave I could be. Also, it was about the only time we got to go out when Hugh wasn't around. I should have listened to my gut then, eh?"

What could Vicky say to that? She remained silent.

The talk of Jessica changed Serj's demeanor. He scowled and sped up as he moved through the shop. Vicky picked up her pace to keep up with him. They jumped obstructions, ducked a couple, and swerved across the littered floor as they both avoided making any loud noises.

Once they got to the back of the store, Serj stopped, slipped his rucksack from his back, ripped the zip open on it, and pulled some door locks from the shelf in front of him.

After he'd put several in, he held one up to Vicky. She took the packet to get a closer look. A cardboard back with a plastic sealed front, the heavy-duty lock weighed about the same as a bag of sugar. It had six keys in the pack too.

"One key each and a spare," Vicky said as she thought about Home's five guards.

"Exactly." Serj took the lock back from Vicky and slipped it into his bag then did the zip up. "I've got eight locks in here."

"*Eight?*"

"If anything goes wrong with me fitting one, I want to make sure I don't have to come back."

A loud scream came from the McDonald's, louder than all the others. Vicky's heart jumped and she looked at Serj before she turned her attention to the front of the shop.

"They sound like they've caught something." Serj's whisper carried through the dark space.

"We need to hurry," Vicky said.

However, before she could move off, she heard a wet squelch. It sounded like a large pig eating slop. When Serj looked at Vicky, she pressed her finger to her lips.

Serj nodded.

Although she'd held onto her bow for the entire time, Vicky raised it again, pressing the stock into her shoulder. She checked her knife. She then took slow and deliberate steps toward the sound.

Once she'd drawn close to a nearby shelving unit, the huge metal rack still upright, she peered around it and froze. On the ground just a couple of metres from her, hidden behind some of the store's furniture, crouched the ravenous form of a diseased child eating a dead dog. Boy or girl, Vicky couldn't tell. Most of them had lank, greasy hair now, and because it had its back to her, she had no idea of its gender. Not that it mattered. The diseased weren't human anyway.

A blank and glassy stare sat in the dead dog's eyes. Its mouth lolled open and its pink tongue lay along the ground. Like a Komodo dragon consumed with its feast, the child seemed oblivious to them watching it.

Another scream outside and Vicky jumped clean off the

ground. Several slow breaths helped her find her composure again.

Serj moved beside Vicky and raised his axe, but she shook her head at him. Instead, she shifted the crossbow until it sat as securely as she could get it into her shoulder and stared at the mass of greasy black hair on the back of the kid's head. Nausea clamped her stomach tight. Diseased or not, she shouldn't be killing children. A clench of her teeth and she pulled the trigger.

Thwack! The bolt embedded in the back of the kid's skull with a pop. It sent an explosion of red through the front of its face and against the white wall. The kid remained upright for a second before it slumped face first into the dead dog's exposed intestines.

For the next few moments Vicky panted as she stared down at it. She then stepped around the shelves, trying not to knock them. When she got to the dead and messy kid, her throat pinched as she started to heave from the stench. She tried to breathe through her mouth and pulled the bolt from the carnage. After she'd wiped it on the kid's clothes, Vicky loaded it back into her crossbow, looked at the glisten of blood on its shaft, and said, "Right, let's get the fuck out of here."

Vicky led the way from the shop this time, stopping at a display with shoelaces on it. She slipped one of her shoulders free from her rucksack's strap, pulled it around her side, and tugged the zip open. After she'd stuffed several packs in, Serj said, "Why so many?"

Vicky looked down at her boots and then Serj's. The laces on both of them had seen better days, knotted in several places from where they'd snapped. "I'm sure we're not the only ones that need them." She stuffed more into her bag. "Also, when we have the keys to give out, I'll want to tie mine around my neck. I know Flynn will need to too. He'll lose it otherwise. Don't tell him I said that though."

Serj laughed. When he fell quiet again, Vicky listened to the distant screams of the diseased in the McDonald's outside. "Come on," she said. "Let's get the fuck out of here."

Chapter Seven

Once she'd stepped outside the shop, Vicky looked over at the McDonald's again. The wind blew into her face as she stared across the abandoned high street. The sun had lowered in the cloudless blue sky, taking some of the day's heat and leaving shadows behind. Maybe if the McDonald's had windows, it would have been easier to ignore, but as she stood there and listened to the call of the diseased, she couldn't deny she heard the scream of a child. It sounded like a little girl.

Serj appeared next to her, his hand across his brow in a clear attempt to block out the low sun. "How are they still alive?"

Vicky shrugged as she looked at the mosh pit of diseased inside the place. "Dunno. But I'll be fucked if I'm going in there."

"You think we should *leave* them?"

"You think we should go *in*? Have a look, Serj; we won't last two minutes against that crowd. It would be suicide. Why risk our lives when theirs are already lost?"

"You don't know that."

"I'm prepared to make an educated guess. Besides, do you have a plan to rescue them?"

Serj didn't say anything; instead he moved along the line of shops closer to the packed McDonald's. The rest of the town seemed abandoned, but Vicky checked about regardless and reached down to touch the knife on her hip. At least one of them had to be careful.

An old fried chicken shop, a fish and chip shop, a coffee shop … as Vicky passed each one after Serj, she looked into the mess inside. They'd all been turned over and all of them seemed free of diseased.

Another charity shop sat at the end of the row. The British Red Cross, it looked to have been mostly left alone. Not even scavengers wanted the shit they tried to sell. What use were books and DVDs now?

Serj got to the shop first and Vicky stepped up beside him a few seconds later. The place smelled of dust and rot. The wooden window frames looked to have collapsed a long time ago and flakes of the damp wood lay scattered on the ground.

They had a clearer view of McDonald's from where they stood and Vicky drew a sharp breath to see the source of the screaming child. What looked like a family of four had barricaded the stairs to the first floor. For now, it kept the diseased penned in on the lower level. Hard to tell from the distance, but it looked to her like a mum, dad, and two daughters. Although like she'd discovered with the dead kids, long hair didn't denote gender anymore. Regardless, the youngest looked to be about ten, the other one about fourteen. Neither of them would see adulthood.

"They must have raided the army surplus store," Serj said. "Other than clothes, they have nothing left in there."

The entire family wore camouflaged gear. "Yeah, I'd say so too. I doubt they have any military experience. They look about as well trained as Hugh."

"Maybe they've been door kicking in Mogadishu too."

Vicky smiled for a second before she looked back at the McDonald's. Hard to maintain her mirth with the sight in front of them.

"We *need* to help them," Serj said.

"They're all right," Vicky replied. "They have the diseased contained."

At that moment, a large diseased man climbed over one of the tables the family was using as a barricade. The dad looked to have an axe like Serj, which he planted in the head of the creature before he threw it back over into the crowd trying to get to them.

"You were saying?" Serj said.

The mum abandoned the others and ran up the stairs. When she appeared at one of the windows on the first floor, Vicky grabbed a handful of Serj's shirt and pulled him back.

"What are you doing?" Serj asked.

"That woman might have seen us." Vicky checked the knife on her hip.

"So what?"

"So *what*? What if she starts screaming at us and alerts that mob to our presence? Look, Serj, I admire that you want to help people out, but you need to take your head out of your arse. We can't beat that crowd."

When a female voice called out, Vicky's stomach sank. "Hey, you! Please help us."

Vicky clamped her jaw shut and shook her head as she glared at Serj.

"*Please*," the woman called again.

Serj stepped forward and Vicky grabbed him. Although taller than her, he cowered slightly in response to her growl. "Don't make me fuck you up. You may be the leader of Home, but that means fuck all out here."

When Vicky heard voices out in the street, she encouraged Serj to step back with a gentle push and slowly poked her head around the corner. Where she'd expected the woman in McDonald's to be looking at her, she found her looking the other way. A crowd of people—mostly men—walked down the street. They carried an array of handheld weapons from bats to machetes, and moved in a line like riot police. Maybe twenty of them, they would give most packs of diseased a good fight.

Serj moved forward next to her and poked his head around the corner too. "I think they've found their saviours," Vicky said.

"You think?"

"Either way, I ain't fighting the diseased *and* them. You can if you like, but you're on your own."

Without consulting Serj, Vicky moved away from the corner and ran in the direction of the road they'd entered the town on. She checked her knife at her hip as she looked into the shops again. The sooner they got away from the place, the better. Fuck knew who the people were, but she didn't have much interest in finding out.

Chapter Eight

Vicky stood in line with the other guards as Serj addressed them, his voice echoing in the enclosed space of Home's foyer. "You all have a key now."

Each gold key had been threaded on a shoelace. Better to give it to Flynn that way than single him out as the one who needed it around his neck like a ten-year-old would. He and Vicky still hadn't spoken much.

Serj walked along the line and handed them out one by one. When Vicky saw Flynn slip the key over his neck, she couldn't help but smile.

"It's crazy that we've had to get some of the kids standing guard for hours so they can let us back in. Now we can do it ourselves. We also have a spare just in case." Serj pointed at the key hanging from a nail on the wall. It hung close to the siren Hugh used to use when they kicked people out. They wouldn't use that again. "That key *mustn't* be removed."

Scoop snorted a laugh as she pulled her dreadlocks back and tied them into a ponytail. "Is that why it says 'key must not be removed' above it?"

For the second time in quick succession, Vicky smiled. She liked Scoop; the woman had fire in her belly.

A facetious grin and Serj continued to pace up and down in front of the five guards. "Any key goes missing and you need to tell me straight away. We can't afford to let them get into the wrong hands. I have eight locks and I can put another one in. Replacing the lock is fine. I'd rather do that than have you feel too shy to tell me you've lost it and we get overrun by hostiles one night."

Maybe he hadn't realised it, but Vicky had watched Serj deliver most of his speech to Flynn.

"What?" Flynn said, "You think I'm going to lose a key because I'm young?"

"I didn't say that," Serj replied.

Flynn either didn't hear him or didn't care. "Jesus, Serj, I know how to look after a key. It's not rocket science."

Normally on the receiving end of Flynn's anger, Vicky remained silent and let them work it out.

"I said, 'I *didn't* say that.'" A usually calm man, Serj's face turned red as he stared at Flynn, daring him to carry on. If he needed to bite the young pup to get him back in line, he would.

Flynn fell silent.

If only Vicky had that control. Flynn would have gone at her all night were she Serj at that moment.

"Also, if you're the last of the guards to return home, make sure you bolt the door. But make sure you *are* the last guard home. I'd hate for the door to be locked with someone still outside."

All the while Serj had spoken, rain crashed against the two huge windows that flanked the main door. So much water fell from the sky it cascaded down the glass.

"We're going out today," Serj said. "Vicky and I have something to show you."

Just the thought of it pulled Vicky's stomach tight. What would they think when they saw it?

"We're going out in *that*?" Scoop said.

A nod and Serj continued to pace up and down, his footsteps light against the hard floor. "It's only a bit of rain. Do you all have weapons?"

A glance down the line and Vicky saw that both Flynn and Piotr had baseball bats. Scoop had a hammer, Serj his axe, and Vicky pulled her crossbow from the harness on her back. She held it with both hands.

"Okay," Serj said, slipping the key in the lock and freeing it with a *click*, "let's go."

"Meisha," Scoop called out as she leaned down the stairs into the canteen.

A few seconds later, Meisha appeared, her eyebrows raised in response to the shout.

"We're going out, sweetheart. Mama Bear loves you and I'll be back soon, all right?"

Meisha nodded but didn't respond.

Vicky and Serj had remained inside waiting for Scoop while Flynn and Piotr stepped out into the rain.

After blowing her daughter a kiss, Scoop stepped outside into the downpour.

Vicky and Serj looked at one another. They didn't need to speak about it. The guards would see it all soon enough. A deep breath to settle her anxiety and Vicky followed the others out. God knew how they'd react when they got to the pen.

Chapter Nine

Despite being summer, the rain came down in sheets and Vicky shivered against the breeze. Her clothes were already soaked and they clung to her as she walked through the field's long grass. She'd got so wet her feet squelched in her boots. The familiar anxiety about rotting laces rose up in her and quickly dropped when she looked down at the new ones she'd put in. It would be months before she had to worry about them again.

None of the group said much over the sound of the swishing grass and strong wind. When Vicky glanced at the others, each of them seemed locked in the same battle as her. Tense jaws, heavy scowls, raised shoulders, they all dipped their heads into the stinging and horizontal rain as they pushed on.

Vicky opened her mouth as she walked. An old habit, she tasted the slightly muddy hint of the rain and quenched her thirst with it. When they'd been in the shipping containers, the rain had always been the freshest source of water. But she now had the filtration system at Home.

Piotr finally spoke. It seemed for no other reason than for the sake of speaking. "It's amazing how much has changed in such a short space of time."

The large Russian looked back at Home and Vicky did too. For the first time she looked at the closed front door and knew her fate didn't depend on kids. Not that they'd ever fucked up, but giving anyone that power over her life made her uneasy.

"To think," Piotr said, "just a few weeks back we were panicking about food. We were trying to get things to grow in over-farmed soil, and Hugh had no idea about how we could improve it. I thought we'd run out. Jessica dying has forced so much change."

Vicky winced and watched the large Russian clamp his hand across his mouth. It muffled his words when he said, "I'm so sorry, Serj. I didn't mean to mention her name or for it to sound that way."

"It's fine," Serj said, scowling as he looked away from the group. He offered a petulant, "I don't care."

A particularly strong gust of wind crashed into Vicky's right side, shoving her a few stumbling steps to the left. The continuous onslaught of the cold rain had turned one side of her face numb. She now felt every stinging drop as if it rained nails.

"We may be outnumbered by Moira's community," Serj said.

The others looked at him, confusion crushing their faces. Although Vicky knew exactly where he was going with it.

He then added, "I don't know how many people they have there; none of us do."

"Yet Stuart keeps asking you," Flynn said to Vicky and giggled. None of the others laughed, so Vicky gave the blushing boy a smile. Piotr and Scoop seemed to get Serj had something important to say from his tone, even if his words hadn't made much sense.

"What we do know, however, is that we need an army on our side," Serj continued. "We can win against them with an army. We need a resilient group that are ready to attack and hopefully able to overwhelm Moira and her lot. They won't know what's hit them when we send them in."

"Aren't you being a bit hopeful calling the people at Home *an army*?" Piotr asked.

Before Serj could respond, the first sounds of the penned diseased rode the winds towards them. Piotr raised his bat and dropped into a defensive hunch. A second later, Scoop and Flynn raised their weapons too.

When Vicky saw Piotr step in front of Flynn, a pang twisted through her chest. But she didn't say anything. It should be a good thing Flynn had someone looking out for him. Even if that someone wasn't her.

Vicky reached across and put a hand on Flynn's forearm to encourage him to lower his bat.

Confusion stared back at her.

"Trust me," she said, "you won't need to fight."

Flynn ignored her, and so he should. For the past decade, the sound of the diseased meant danger. Vicky pulled her hand away from him and let him grip his weapon and scan the distance for signs of the horrible fuckers.

"I've just had a thought," Scoop said as she walked with a hunch and scowled at the horizon. "If we get chased, how will we get back into Home quickly?"

"We won't get chased," Serj said.

"Can't you hear that?" Scoop replied.

Serj shook his head. "We won't get chased. Trust me."

The looks from Flynn, Scoop, and Piotr suggested they thought Serj had lost the plot. One by one they looked at Vicky for backup. She didn't give it to them. Just a few more paces and they'd crest the top of the small hill.

Serj stopped at that moment and turned to the others. "What we have here," he said, and then backed up a few paces to the top of the hill, "is a group of expendables." He introduced the scene as if opening a fictional door with his left arm.

To be fair to Flynn, he articulated it best as they all moved forward to see what lay beyond the hill. The boy pulled his sodden hair from his eyes and said, "What the fuck?"

Chapter Ten

It didn't matter how many times Vicky crested the small hill, whenever she saw the pen she nearly froze. Over two hundred diseased stretched out before them. All of them had chased her at one point or another in the past few months and, if she looked hard enough, she could recognise every one of their horrible faces.

Vicky pushed on, fighting against her leaden limbs and the stinging onslaught of the rain. *They're penned in; they can't get out.* Regardless of how many times she told herself that, she couldn't get over her fear when she saw the horrible bastards.

"The fuck?" Flynn said as if his first expletive didn't quite hit the mark.

"Vicky and I have been gathering these for several weeks now," Serj said.

Vicky noticed Flynn stare across at her in her peripheral vision, but she didn't look back. Another thing she'd kept from him. He had every right to be pissed off with her, but they didn't need to address it now.

Serj raised his voice over the sound of the wind and rain. "We've been luring them in and gathering them up."

"Because life isn't dangerous enough for you already?" Flynn said.

Vicky hated when he got in these moods. He'd do anything for an argument. She could really do without mediating for the hot-headed boy today. Fortunately, she didn't need to because Serj ignored him and continued.

"We're going to set them loose on Moira's community."

Piotr pointed down at the pen. "*This* is your army?"

"Yep."

"Total cannon fodder," Vicky said. "We don't have to worry about their well-being and they can put a serious dent in Moira's gang."

"How do you know?" Scoop said. "You said you don't know how many of them are down there."

At first Vicky didn't have an answer. Then she said, "We don't know *exactly* how many, but even if we assume the worst, there are enough diseased here to seriously damage them. Also, don't forget there are a good twenty to thirty people in the prison on our side too. It'll be chaos when we send these things over the top. That'll work in our favour."

When none of the others spoke, Serj led them toward the pen and closer to the stench of rot.

As they followed behind, Flynn moved close to Vicky. Just by the way he held himself, she could feel his anger, but before he could vent it, the shrill call of a diseased rang out. Paranoid for Flynn's safety, Vicky raised her bow and jumped in front of the boy.

Serj turned to look at her. "It came from *within* the pen. There's nothing to worry about."

Flynn spoke beneath his breath so only Vicky could hear him. "Yeah, and I can look after myself, *thanks*."

The gunmetal grey sky and fierce rain made the pen of diseased all the more ominous. Unlike the guards, who all flinched or covered their faces against the elements, the diseased seemed oblivious to it as they stood like statues and stared at the approaching group.

Serj guided them along the side of the fence. "As you can see, they're secure in here. This pen was already set up to obviously hold some kind of livestock. Because these fuckers can't climb, we're fairly confident they won't get out."

The fence resembled many Vicky had seen before. It had upright poles with two horizontal wooden bars between each one. Maybe they'd kept horses in the pen before the diseased. Fuck knew, but with the chicken wire all the way around, it served as the perfect enclosure for the horrible bastards.

Once they'd rounded the first bend, they had to get slightly closer to the fence. With the river on one side and the pen on the other, the walkway narrowed, but not to the point where it put any of them in danger. The diseased reached out, and although it felt like they could grab one of them, Vicky had been down here enough times to know they couldn't. It didn't stop Piotr, Scoop, and Flynn from recoiling from their grasping hands though.

"We might try to get a few more in here before we release them," Serj said.

"And how do you know they'll go to Moira's complex rather than ours?" Scoop asked.

"I'm going to run ahead of them," Vicky said.

Scoop's face fell slack. "You're *what*?"

Before Vicky could reply, the screech of another diseased called out. It sounded much like the one earlier, the one who'd made Vicky jump. And now she heard it again, she looked up and her breath quickened. As did her words. "It's not in the pen, Serj."

The creature sprinted for them and screamed. Dried bloody eyes fixed on the group as it gnashed at the air with its wide mouth and reached out in front of itself. It moved with its clumsy yet fast gait and screamed again.

Before any of them had time to react, the monster got to Serj at the front of the group. He ducked under its swinging arms.

A step later and it came to Vicky. She dodged to the side and knocked into Flynn behind her. She watched the diseased but heard Flynn scream. Her body locked tight when his yell ended with a splash of water. Cold dread sank through her.

The diseased had totally left Vicky's mind and she had only a vague awareness of Piotr and Scoop beating it down. Instead, she turned to look into the river where Flynn had fallen in. She couldn't see him. One quick check around and Vicky dived in after him.

Chapter Eleven

The tide grabbed Vicky as soon as she broke the surface, and the coldness of the water drew the air from her body. It turned her over as if she were dirty washing on a spin cycle. She tumbled so fast she barely knew where the sky and the ground were. One second she saw gunmetal grey and felt the stinging lash of rain above her, and the next her face went under, where she saw the brown muddy churn of the river.

As if goaded by the storm, the river turned into a wild and frenzied beast. Vicky swore she heard it growl as it barreled along.

When she got her head above the water for more than a few seconds, Vicky gasped a deep breath. As she fought against the tide to remain upright, she scanned for Flynn. She couldn't see him. She opened her mouth to call out and inhaled a huge gulp of muddy water.

Vicky vomited it straight back out again. It came up as cleanly as it had gone down, wiping its feet by leaving a slightly gritty bile on the back of her throat. Other than that, she recovered quickly.

Despite the chaos around her, Vicky heard a splash of water accompanied by a loud gasp. She saw Flynn break the surface, his mouth opened wide as he breathed before he disappeared again. Although a strong swimmer, even she found it hard to stay afloat.

In her desperation to see Flynn, Vicky dipped her head into the murky and rushing depths, but her search revealed nothing. The brown churn pulled the mud up from the riverbed and turned everything into a cloudy soup.

The banks on either side stood at least a metre higher than the water level, so even if Flynn did get over to one, he'd have no chance of climbing out, especially with the strong current dragging at them like it did. The only way he'd get out of there was if Vicky saved him. But what else could she do other than watch the spot she'd seen him in last?

The heavy rain dappled the water. When added to the choppy flow, it seemed quite possible Flynn could appear for a second, and Vicky would miss him amongst the chaos already there. There had to be a better way to find him. She dropped beneath the surface again.

A couple of blinks against the misty fugue and Vicky's sight cleared a little to reveal something on the riverbed. When she recognised what she saw, she gasped so hard she inhaled another gulp, coughing instantly as she fought to return to the surface.

Once Vicky had her head above water, she vomited for a second time. It didn't come as easily as the first. The thick rush of muddy liquid caught in her throat and momentarily choked her. Another hot rush of vomit, chunky and acidic, forced the first lot out and she found her breath again.

Vicky might have stopped choking, but it didn't change what she'd seen beneath her; a carpet of diseased lay on the bottom of the river. They'd clearly tried to cross it and failed, hundreds, if not thousands of times. They looked to be drowned, but what if some of them still lived? Maybe they'd only just fallen in and they lay in wait for an errant limb to drag, pull under, and bite into. Maybe they had Flynn already.

Another particularly strong surge ran through the river and it flipped Vicky onto her back, forcing her to look up at the cloudy sky and bear the sting of the rain against her cheeks.

Hearing the splash of breaking water ahead, Vicky fought to pull herself back over onto her front. Time seemed to slow when she couldn't breathe moments ago, but when she caught a glance of Flynn, it moved at light speed, the boy breaking through the water, flailing for some kind of control over his situation, and then vanishing beneath the surface again. She heard his bark of a breath. If she didn't hurry, he'd surely drown.

Hopefully the diseased weren't active on the riverbed. Although what did it matter at that point? Vicky hardly had any other options. She fought to ride the currents, doing breaststroke with the flow of the river to try to catch up with Flynn.

Each powerful stroke clawed at Vicky's stamina. The sound of her own struggle echoed through her head.

Flynn burst up from the depths again. No more than a metre separated them, but despite reaching across the gap, it stretched just that little bit too far. For the briefest second, Vicky and Flynn shared a look. Wild panic sat in Flynn's eyes and she wanted to tell him it would be okay. However, before she could do anything, he'd slipped beneath the surface again.

Vicky dived straight after Flynn, her tired limbs on fire as she fought to get to him. Two strong strokes before she reached out and caught the back of his jacket and pulled him in. The long, slim form of a boy yet to be a man came easily enough for her to hold him beneath his armpits.

Despite the ease with which Vicky pulled Flynn in, she struggled to get him up to the surface. For the briefest second it felt like she might not make it and her panicked pulse hammered through her skull. With her legs dangling down, she imagined a clawing hand grabbing her ankle and dragging on them both. The fear weakened her kick and her lungs felt ready to burst. Then she looked down at the rotting mass of swollen bodies, and she found an extra spurt of energy. She pumped her legs, forcing them both up.

Once they broke the surface again, Vicky rolled Flynn so he faced the grey sky. She put her right arm underneath his right armpit and reached across his chest. She used her other arm and legs to swim as she guided them to the side. A look over her shoulder and she saw a lower part of the riverbank. A place where they could get out.

The rain continued to lash Vicky's face, pebble-dashing her to the point where she nearly closed her eyes against the sting of the pregnant drops.

When she reached the riverbank, Vicky fought against her desire to flop the second she hit land. There could be hundreds of diseased ready to reach up to them. They had to get away from the water.

Heavy pants rocked Vicky's entire frame and she opened her mouth wide to breathe. The muddy riverbank tugged on her every step, fighting her as she dragged Flynn up through the liquid earth. Each movement squelched, even above the hammering of her pulse and the lashing of the rain, and Flynn's limp heels dragged through the clogged ground.

A few metres from the water, Vicky fell into the mud with a loud *slurp*. She let go of Flynn but fought her desire to fall limp with exhaustion. Instead, she rested up on one elbow and watched him as he lay pale and still.

Before she could do anything else, Flynn vomited, so Vicky rolled him into the recovery position and patted his back. Another heave and water rushed out of him. "There, there, you're doing so well. Keep clearing your lungs, mate."

Close to collapse herself, the scream of a diseased roused Vicky. She looked over her shoulder at the hideous woman. She seemed to be no more than thirty years old and looked like she'd only recently turned. Her clothes hadn't started to rot on her body yet, and the claret lines running from her eyes glistened with fresh blood. Her light blonde hair and pale complexion made the angry streaks of red on her face stand out from a mile away.

With her crossbow unloaded but still strapped to her back, Vicky yelled as she used all of her dwindled strength to yank it free. As she spun around to face the diseased woman again, she launched her weapon. The crossbow spun through the air, covering the distance between them in an instant and connecting with the centre of the diseased woman's face. The impact drove the woman backwards and knocked her to the ground.

Vicky jumped to her feet and ran at the woman, removing her knife from her hip as she moved. Somewhere between a stumble and a leap, she dived at the diseased freak and drove her blade into her skull. It popped through the bone as it sank into the top of the woman's head.

Several convulsive kicks and the woman fell limp while Vicky remained on top of her.

For the next few seconds, Vicky watched the downed diseased to be sure she wouldn't move again. She then rolled off her and fell into the thick mud on her back.

Once she'd slightly recovered, Vicky stared up at the blackening sky. The storm seemed to be getting worse.

Chapter Twelve

Vicky walked back down to where she'd left Flynn and held her muddy hand out to him. The boy took it, his own grip as caked as hers. A hard tug and she pulled him from the cloying mud around his bottom. He came up with a wet *squelch*. Although Vicky wanted to hug him, she held back. She'd promised she wouldn't mother him anymore and she needed to stick by that.

Vicky walked through the mud, with Flynn beside her. Every time she put her foot down, the thirsty ground gripped it and almost didn't let go. She looked up the hill in front of them to see the other Home guards waiting at the top.

"Do you think they followed us down?" Flynn asked. He still looked pale, but at least he had the strength to move. They needed to get back to Home before they rested.

"It certainly looks that way," Vicky replied.

The rushing body of water behind them whooshed as it tore along, but the farther they moved away from it, the more its sound got buried beneath the noise of the heavy rain. It fell so hard Vicky locked in a permanent wince against its lashing.

It might have only been a small incline, but with the weather battering her, and exhausted from her struggle to save Flynn, Vicky's legs shook with each step up it. A particularly strong gust of wind hit her and she stumbled sideways, nearly falling as she fought to free her feet from the mud to keep up with her quick steps.

As they passed the downed diseased, Vicky looked across at Flynn and saw him staring at the thing. The woman's light blonde hair lay as a halo, sprawled out around her. It rested in the soaked mud, blood from her wound turning the surface water pink. Her mouth hung open as if she still released a death call, and her bloody eyes were spread so wide Vicky shuddered at the sight of the two crimson orbs.

The rain continued, unrelenting, and Vicky looked at Flynn again to see his frown against the elements. "At least we can't get any wetter," she said.

Flynn forced a tight-lipped and humourless smile.

Each step up the hill took a little more of Vicky's energy. It seemed like the next one would be the one where she fell and the guards would have to carry her. Yet she managed to keep going, her entire body weight slamming down on the ground with each heavy footfall.

Flynn's tone changed when he spoke again, his jaw clenched tight. "I think it's fucking *mental* to keep so many diseased penned in."

Vicky squinted against the hard rain and looked at the red-faced boy. She saw the insecurity behind his anger, the shifting of his eyes from side to side, the stoop of humiliation. "It wasn't the diseased in the pen that attacked us."

"No, but they attracted that one over. If the pen didn't exist, that diseased wouldn't have been there, and even if it was, we would have been able to see it from a mile away." Flynn left his hair in his eyes as he glared rage at Vicky.

Vicky didn't reply to him as they stepped from the mud onto the grassy incline. The ground remained hard from a warm summer, and walking suddenly became a hell of a lot easier. Although, if the rain continued to fall like it currently did, it wouldn't take much to turn everywhere into a boggy mess. They could really do with solid ground underfoot when they tried to lead the diseased to Moira's community. A look up at the sky and she saw breaks of blue in the black cloud. Hopefully, it would pass soon.

"But you can see how we could take down Moira's army with them, right?" Vicky said. "If we can avoid a fight that will see many of our people killed, that has to be a good thing. I'd rather not die. How about you?"

A sharp shrug and Flynn looked away as if searching for diseased on the horizon. "I just think it's bloody dangerous. It could go wrong in so many ways."

Vicky closed the distance between them so the others wouldn't hear her. "It's not your fault you can't swim. There's no shame in it."

Flynn spun around to face her, his brown eyes narrowed, his lips pulled back to reveal his yellowing teeth. "No, but it is *your* fault. Why didn't you teach me? I think you avoided doing it because you like me feeling vulnerable. It makes *you* feel useful."

The words drove a blow to Vicky's gut and she balked, but before she could reply, Flynn sped up and marched away from her. He headed straight for Piotr. The large Russian looked down the hill at her for a moment, a twist of pity on his large features. He then focused on the boy and dipped a nod at him.

Vicky sighed. If she couldn't be the one to help him, at least Flynn had someone in his corner.

Chapter Thirteen

Vicky shivered and hugged herself for warmth, anxiety tying knots in her stomach. Maybe she shouldn't have come out alone. The temperature had dropped unusually low for the middle of the night, especially for June. Were it not for the moon running a silver highlight over her wild surroundings, it would have been much harder to navigate the landscape.

A strong wind tore across the open grasslands, carrying the rotten smell of the diseased with it. The scent whispered to Vicky of what could be waiting in the darkness for her. But she couldn't focus on what she couldn't see. Of course there were diseased around, but she hadn't even heard them yet, so they obviously weren't that close.

Vicky stood far enough back from the chain-link fence to remain concealed in the shadows. At least she expected she did. How could she truly tell? Without the ability to look out of the cage with the prisoners in it, she could only speculate on what they saw.

No one from Home knew Vicky had come here. Since she'd moved Flynn to a different room and they put a key lock on the front door, she could come and go unnoticed, especially in the middle of the night. If she'd have told anyone of her plans, they would have tried to come with her or stop her. No way would she let Flynn come out, and Serj needed to stay at Home as their leader. Besides, she'd be more inconspicuous alone.

The chill on the breeze worked its way into Vicky's bones and her entire body clamped as tight as her stomach. Although maybe the shake running through her had more to do with returning to this awful place. To come back to Moira's community so willingly bordered on madness, but she had to do it. They had to know what they were up against when everything kicked off, and the prisoners needed to know they'd be rescued. Besides, everything would be fine as long as none of Moira's lot saw her.

Vicky looked at the small cage they'd held her in when Hugh shoved her down the hill, and her heart rate increased. Whatever happened, she didn't plan on going back into that fucking cell.

The larger cage had about twenty prisoners in it at present. From what Vicky had seen during her short stay, that number fluctuated daily depending on Moira's mood.

Vicky needed to step forward and reveal herself, but she needed to pick her move carefully. A group of desperate people, if the wrong one saw her first, they'd call out and it would be game over for all of them.

When Vicky saw the man from the farm, she moved alongside the cage until she stood as close to him as she could without stepping forward. If any of them could keep their voice down, she guessed it would be him. Hopefully he could encourage the others to do the same.

Large tufts protruded from the lumpy ground surrounding Moira's compound. Either weeds, thistles, or hard, callous-like explosions of grass. Not conducive to an easy getaway, it looked almost as if Moira's influence poisoned the very earth around her.

After a deep breath to still her furious pulse, Vicky hissed at the man she recognised.

He didn't react.

Vicky hissed again.

This time he slowly rotated his head, his eyes half closed. The movement seemed to take a great effort, and once he'd turned his face out toward the darkness, he blinked repeatedly as if trying to ascertain the source of the sound.

Vicky took another step forward.

When the man's eyes widened, Vicky pressed her finger to her lips. Fortunately, he obliged her.

Two quick steps and Vicky closed the distance between them. She did her best to hide her reaction to the foul smell of human waste coming from the cage. They probably felt ashamed enough already; she didn't need to make it worse. The rucksack on her back had weighed heavy with food and water, and now she'd got to the man unnoticed, she felt relief to roll the heavy pack from her shoulders and lower it to the ground. She bit her bottom lip as she opened the bag, willing the zip to remain quiet while the man from the farm urged silence from the others.

There had been bigger bottles at Home and it might have been more practical to bring them, but Vicky knew how small the holes in the fence were.

Each bottle—just about small enough to fit through the gaps—popped and cracked as Vicky forced them in.

Seventeen bottles in total, Vicky's heart galloped after she'd got them all through. Adrenaline raced through her veins, accelerating her pulse and making her hands shake as she passed the other supplies through to the man. Carrots, cucumbers, cooked potatoes, and a small amount of cured rabbit before she'd exhausted her stash. "Sorry it's not more," she said, "but I'll be back again, I promise."

Wide and tired eyes stared at Vicky from sunken faces. Stray dogs on death row, every one of the prisoners looked to her as their saviour. Every one of them begged to be taken home.

"Listen," Vicky said, "we have a plan and we'll get you all out of here. A day or two longer and we're going to storm this place, so be ready, yeah?"

None of the prisoners spoke. Hope seemed to lighten their features, but mistrust clearly fought against their optimism. If life with Moira had taught them anything, it would have been that hope didn't exist in their world. Besides, a few days could be too long for many of them. As if answering Vicky's thoughts, the low murmur of the diseased in the pit in the courtyard called out to her. They were hungry for more meat.

As Vicky watched the people eat, apparently oblivious to the blood-curdling sound of the diseased in the pit, she turned to the man from the farm. "I never got your name."

"Aaron."

"Just Aaron?"

"What does a surname matter now? My dad was an arsehole; he can keep it."

Vicky nodded. "Well, Aaron, I'm Vicky. I promise I'll be back for you. You've survived this long, I'm confident you'll do okay."

"I'm glad *you* are."

Neither spoke as the wind seemed to pick up. Vicky looked over her shoulder into the darkness. If a horde attacked now, she could do nothing to stop them. By the time she saw them, it would be too late. She also looked toward the section where the guards hung out. Anxiety shimmered through her.

Aaron cut through Vicky's thoughts. "Now let me ask you something."

"Go on."

"Why should I wait for you to come back?" He stroked his stubbled chin, his cheeks so withdrawn his thin skin did nothing to conceal his skull beneath. "I reckon Moira would give a lot to someone who handed you back to her." His green eyes lit up. "Like, I dunno, *freedom* maybe?"

The people around Aaron stirred, but Vicky focused on the man from Home. Any noise and he could alert both the guards and the diseased. Any noise and she might not see the morning.

"I mean, you're the one who got away. You and I both know that will never sit well with her and she would do a *lot* to right that wrong."

Vicky wanted to speak, but the silence of the evening seemed to reach into her lungs and steal her words. Quickened breaths and a dry throat and she stared at Aaron. As much as she wanted to reach for the knife on her hip, she didn't. She'd come to rescue them, not kill them.

Aaron's green eyes narrowed and a wonky grin spread across his withdrawn face. "I'm guessing you don't have a good reason, then?" He drew a deep breath as if to call out.

Chapter Fourteen

Despite her hammering heart, Vicky fought to keep her voice level and just got her words out before Aaron could shout anything. "When have you seen Moira reward anyone? *Especially* a prisoner?"

Silence met her question and some of the people around Aaron shifted as if the ground had grown uncomfortable to stand on.

"Exactly. At least with me there are no conditions. When I come to rescue you, you won't belong to me or anyone else." Vicky looked at the others. "And I'll free *all* of you. So if you want to call me out—if you want to jeopardise the only opportunity these people around you may have of escaping—then go for it. I'll be dead and so will any chance of their freedom." She stared at Aaron, and the gathered crowd seemed to hold their breath. From the looks on their faces, they clearly understood their fate rested in the palms of his long and bony hands. They also looked ready to lynch him if need be.

Another check over both shoulders and Vicky couldn't see any movement around her. Not that it meant her surroundings were clear, but she had to take it at face value and pray for good luck. She felt for her knife on her hip.

"Right, I'm glad we're on the same page, then," Vicky finally said when Aaron offered no response. The determined set to his face had vanished. "I'm prepared to forget your threat and move on, but don't try me again. I swear I will let you *all* rot in here. Now, give me those water bottles back. We can't have Moira twigging that you've all had a drink. She'll be sure to punish anyone who's gone against her rule."

One by one the people in the cage passed the empty bottles to Vicky. They crunched even louder on the way back through. Each one went into her open backpack, the weight of it considerably lighter than it had been on the way over.

Vicky shouldered her pack again and stared at Aaron. "*Please* trust me. I need to suss this place out so we have the best chance of toppling it. If I bust you out now, we won't stand a chance. Half of you are so weak you can barely stand. Let me do this my way and we'll come back with an army. I have the people who will fight for you if you let them."

"And in the meantime?" Aaron asked. The prisoners around him moved forward as if silently asking the same question.

"You wait. I know you don't want to hear that, but it's all I have. I promise you"—Vicky looked at the others—"I promise you all, I don't take your incarceration lightly. I'll get back to you as quickly as I can."

Many of the group nodded, and when Vicky focused on Aaron again, she saw his animosity melt away with lethargic resignation.

Chapter Fifteen

Vicky stepped back a few paces into the veil of night. Still able to see the prisoners, she could tell by the way they peered into the darkness—their hollow stares vague—that she'd disappeared from their view.

The lighter load in Vicky's backpack made it easier for her to move. She walked over the hard and tufty ground, the bitter chill in the air cutting to her bones. A clamped stomach and jaw did nothing to fight the frigid snap.

Once Vicky passed the part of Moira's camp where they kept the prisoners, she came upon the guards' area. A particularly long brick building divided the two sections. Although she couldn't see it from her current position, she knew there to be a walkway connecting the two areas on the opposite side of the complex.

Three other buildings took up most of the space. They ran around the outside and had a courtyard in the centre of them. The corners of the complex had been finished off with fences where the buildings didn't budge up against one another, except for one corner, which had a large square building in it. Different from the others, it looked to be a communal area rather than sleeping quarters.

Light shone from the large square building. Not only light, but the sound of voices came from it too. Vicky hadn't noticed them when talking to Aaron, but now she'd got closer, they became much easier to hear. Maybe they kept the noise down for fear of attracting the diseased. Even a crowd as seemingly in control and fortified as this lot lived in fear of the monsters in the wild.

Because only a small amount of light spilled out of the communal hut, it made it hard for Vicky to see the structure in the middle of the courtyard, but she could see something stood there. In silhouette, it looked to be a large box. Rectangular in shape, it stood about eight feet tall and twice as wide—maybe another cage. When she squinted against the darkness, she saw something inside it move and gasped.

Light rushed out of the communal building through the courtyard when someone opened the door. Clearly a fire inside, the orange glow of it seeped out into the night, animating any shadow it cast. Vicky jumped back and dropped down into a crouch behind a bush to her right.

Hidden about as well as she could be at that moment, Vicky looked at the jail in the courtyard and her heart sank. A sudden gust of wind ripped across the open landscape and crashed into her. It rocked her where she crouched as she stared at the people in the cage.

The door closed again and shut off the light, but she'd already seen them. A family of four huddled in one corner. A mum, dad, and two daughters. At least Vicky assumed they were a family. And if they weren't before, this world had clearly turned them into one. Of the two children, one looked to be about ten years old and the other about fourteen. They all wore army camouflage.

Vicky thought about when she'd watched the group in the town walk up the road towards McDonald's. The group she'd hoped would become saviours for the family of four.

When the door to the communal area swung open for a second time, Vicky saw another person in the cage with them. A scruffy man, he looked to be in his late fifties, but she couldn't really tell from her current position and in the poor light. At opposite ends of the cage from one another, the two parties were clearly divided by hostility.

As with Aaron and the prisoners next door, Vicky couldn't do anything to help. Not at that moment anyway. She had to hurry the fuck up and come back with the diseased. The sooner she did it, the better.

It would serve no other purpose to wait around, other than to maybe understand how many guards they were up against, but that could take hours. Instead, Vicky slowly stood up and stepped backwards into the darkness.

As she crept away, Vicky looked between where she headed and Moira's complex. The tufty ground threatened to trip her. When she'd got far enough back, she filled her lungs with a deep inhale and ran back towards Home.

Chapter Sixteen

Vicky crossed the canteen with leaden legs. She'd only come back from Moira's community a few hours previously, and she couldn't sleep a wink when she had. She thought of the family in one cage and the prisoners in the other. Their lives depended on her. She couldn't tell the guards about them because she'd have to admit to going to Moira's community. If she did that, they'd either try to come with her next time or try to stop her; she had to be able to go again because her intel on the place could prove invaluable.

The blue crash mats sank beneath Vicky's steps as she crossed them to the seating on the other side of the space. The air smelled of boiled cabbage, not that they'd served boiled cabbage every day since she'd been there. The scent whisked her back to her school canteen every time she smelled it.

Vicky looked at her feet to avoid making eye contact with anyone. The chatter of tens of voices swelled through the place and turned into a white noise in the high ceiling above her.

A quick look up at the screens and she saw they gave their usual glimpse of the outside world. The occasional diseased ran past, but Vicky paid them little mind. They had enemies much more dangerous than the diseased, and she'd seen what they did to people.

Flynn, Serj, Piotr, Scoop, and Scoop's teenage daughter, Meisha, all sat together. When Vicky drew close, Meisha got to her feet, hugged her mum, and headed to a different table. Before she could get away, Scoop reached out and grabbed her arm, pulling her back in for another firm hug.

Vicky sat down and Serj pushed a plate with a bun on it and a cup of water across the white Formica surface to her. Piotr offered her a tight-lipped smile, but Flynn completely ignored her.

"It's scary, isn't it?" Vicky said to Scoop as she watched Meisha join some people at another table. "She's growing up so quickly."

Scoop beamed a smile at her.

"You must be so proud."

"She's a strong young woman," Scoop said. "Although, she's not always been that way. It's how I got my nickname, you know?"

A bite on the rough bread and Vicky chewed it. Bland, but it filled a hole. What she'd give for some jam. She pushed the half-chewed bread to the side of her mouth and smiled as she said, "You mean you weren't christened *Scoop*?"

Scoop laughed. "When Meisha was a kid, all she'd say to me was *scoop, scoop, scoop*." As she looked off into the distance, Scoop smiled and her eyes lost focus. "She wanted me to pick her up, as in *scoop* her up."

"And you always did," Serj said.

A heavy sigh and Scoop nodded. "Yep, I always did."

"That's probably why she's so confident now," Vicky said, taking another bite of the plain bread. "You gave her what she needed as a kid. That's gotta set her up for being a well-balanced adult, right? They know how loved they are and that makes them secure."

A glance over at the table with her daughter and Scoop's stare glazed with tears. "I've tried my best." She laughed and dabbed the corners of her eyes. "My God, look at me! Becoming a mum has made me so soft."

Vicky smiled again. After the night she'd had, Scoop had just shown her exactly what she needed to see. "You're clearly a *great* mum."

"Anyway," Scoop said, "how are you? You look tired. You're normally the first one in here."

"I had a rough night." The image of the family in the cage snapped through her mind and it took all she had not to flinch.

Silence hung for a second as if the group wanted more information from her, but Vicky didn't give it.

Serj finally spoke. "Right, I need to see all of your keys. We need to do regular checks to make sure none of them have gone missing."

One by one, they all pulled their keys from beneath their shirts. Although Vicky had intended for the shoelaces to be used by Flynn, she smiled to see everyone else had adopted the idea too.

Serj checked them all and nodded. "Good. I'll change the locks when I have to, but I'd like to do it as little as possible."

Stifling a yawn as best as she could, Vicky clamped her jaw

shut and watched her world blur in front of her as her eyes welled up. Heavy limbs, heavy eyelids, slow thoughts …

Before Vicky could drift off into a daydream, a scream cut through the place, silencing everyone in the busy area and forcing each head to turn to the entranceway.

A short woman of about five feet four inches screamed again. Her cry rang so shrill it sent stabbing pains into Vicky's ears, and her shoulders tensed in response. She recognised the woman as Sharon Blythe. She'd never seen her cause a fuss before.

Dan—Sharon's husband—stood next to her. Although he didn't shout, he looked equally as distressed.

Serj stood up and called over at them, "What's wrong?"

"They've *taken* them!" Sharon shouted.

"Who's been taken?" Serj said. "What are you talking about?"

"Our *children*! They're *gone*!"

Ice ran through Vicky's veins and she searched the room as if the children would appear. Most people watched the parents with their jaws hanging loose.

"Gone where?" Serj said.

It seemed like a stupid question to Vicky, but she probably wouldn't have asked anything better.

Dan stroked his wife's back as he spoke. "We took them out with us this morning to clean the solar panels." He turned to Vicky and his voice broke when he raised it. "*You* said we should get them used to the outside. Well, we tried to do that and now they've been taken from us."

Fire spread through Vicky's cheeks and her pulse sped up, but she didn't reply to him.

"They've taken all three of them?" Serj said.

One of the reasons why Serj made a better leader than Vicky ever could … he knew the people. He remembered who they all were and how many children they had. He remembered names and minor details. She knew they had kids, but she couldn't remember how many or their genders, let alone their ages. They were young, that much she knew. The youngest was maybe a boy.

"Who took them?" Serj said.

Dan drew a deep breath. "Three men and two women. They knew they had us outnumbered. They got between us and the kids. They had weapons and said they were taking them. We couldn't do anything about it. Three of them held us in one place." He rubbed the swelling on his face. "They whacked me and told us to stay put while the other two took the kids away. They said the kids would have a chance at surviving if we didn't resist."

"Do you know where they've taken them?" Vicky said.

"How the fuck would *I* know?" Dan shook as he shouted. His eyes brimmed with tears and a large vein raised on his forehead. "Do you think I'd be *here* if I knew that?"

"I'm just asking so we can help."

"You've helped enough. None of this would have happened if we hadn't taken them outside."

Vicky wanted to respond—especially as she felt most of the people turn to look at her—but she kept her mouth shut. They had every right to be upset, and she couldn't say anything to change that. Instead, she stood up and headed for one of the corridors out of the canteen. Her footsteps registered as the only sound in the silence.

"Where are you going?" Serj asked. His voice echoed through the cavernous room.

"I'm going to get some weapons and then I'm going to rescue the kids. No way are they taking people from this place. No fucking way."

Although Vicky didn't look back around, she didn't need to; the sound of action behind her clearly came from the guards mobilising. They were in this together.

Chapter Seventeen

Vicky left Home and didn't close the door because the four other guards followed her out. The second she stepped into the warm June sun, she turned around and walked up the hill the door had been built into. She only had one place in her mind: Moira's community. Although what she'd do when she got there …

At the top of the short hill, Vicky looked over the field of solar panels. A sea of black, it always awed her no matter how many times she saw it. How it had remained untouched for so many years … Surely someone had designs to destroy them.

Vicky kept a few steps ahead of the rest of the guards, weaving quickly through the panels as sweat lifted on her face from the combination of effort and heat. The grass had been well trodden from where the residents of Home went outside more often. Although, if she hadn't insisted on it in the first place, the kids would still be okay.

Once through the solar panels, Vicky walked for a few minutes before she saw the next short incline. Butterflies fluttered through her chest. The other side of it plunged down to Moira's fenced-in complex.

A deep breath and Vicky smelled pollen in the air. Never being one for hay fever, she remembered seeing people at this time of year dripping in snot. Although not so much now; maybe it had more to do with pesticides than it did pollen.

The ground on the small hill sat as lumpy and calloused as it did outside Moira's community. Vicky didn't slow down as she scaled it, checking the knife on her hip as she went.

When Vicky crested the top, the sight in front of her drove a mule's kick to her stomach and she stumbled back. A second later, her legs gave way and she crashed down hard against the lumpy ground.

Before the rest of the guards could follow her up, Vicky raised a palm at them and shouted, "Stop!" Although she'd aimed it at all of them, she meant it for Flynn. He didn't need to see this.

The guards did as she instructed.

Turning back to face Moira's community, Vicky's head spun. "W-wait there. Just wait there," she called to the others.

Although Vicky had mobilised quickly, she clearly hadn't done it quickly enough. Why hadn't she headed straight out? In the time it had taken her to get to the weapons room and cross the small distance between the two communities, *this* had happened.

A look at the three forms—the backdrop of Moira's brutal complex behind them—and Vicky cried uncontrollably. All three of them had been crucified.

"How could they do this to *kids*?" Piotr said.

When Vicky looked to either side, she saw all of the guards had made their way up, even Flynn. Sadness, rage, and guilt swirled within her and formed a tight ball in her guts. She directed it all at Flynn. "I told you to *stop*. What are you doing? Why don't you *ever* listen to me?"

"I'm not the only one who didn't listen to you." Flynn looked at Piotr, but the large Russian didn't get involved. He clearly knew when to shut the fuck up.

"I'm getting fed up with it, Flynn. You chuck your weight around all the time and forget you're only *sixteen*. Why do you continue to disregard *everything* I say to you?"

The sides of Flynn's jaw widened and eased from where he clamped and then relaxed it, but he didn't respond. And maybe he'd been right to hold it in. They didn't need a row at that moment.

"Look," Scoop said as she walked toward one of the corpses. He appeared to be the eldest of the three. Vicky didn't know his name.

He had some kind of letter attached to him, nailed through his chest bone with a rusty six-inch nail. At first, Vicky had only glanced at the bodies, but now she looked again, she saw their hands and feet dripping fresh blood from where they'd been recently nailed up. She saw each child had had their eyes gouged out. Streaks of red ran down their faces as if to recreate the diseased look. Huge crude holes had also been dug into their chests, and their hearts had been removed.

Before Vicky could ask Scoop what the letter said, her head spiralled out of control, her stomach bucked, and a hot rush of thick and acidic vomit exploded from her.

Chapter Eighteen

Vicky wiped her mouth with the back of her sleeve and spat the bilious taste of vomit away from her. A line of stringy bile caught on her bottom lip and dribbled down her chin. She wiped for a second time and spat again, her stomach still churning at the sight in front of her.

The wind on the hill picked up and tousled the children's hair, animating the now permanently inanimate. It also tossed the letter nailed into the kid's chest, forcing Scoop to grab it in a pinch as she read it aloud. "This is what happens when you break free. We never had any beef with the people of Home, but she's mugged us off by breaking out. Now we're coming for all of you."

All of the guards looked at Vicky.

It took for Serj to speak up to break the silence. "It's okay; no one blames you. I know I would have busted out given half the chance and I'm sure everyone here would have too."

All of the guards nodded.

Serj pointed down the hill, his hair covering his eyes from where the wind caught it. "That community has been allowed to exist for far too long. We need to put a stop to it. All you've done is force our hand."

Vicky swallowed and nodded several times before she found her voice. Even Serj—their leader in name only—looked at her for their next move. "We need to pull those kids down," she said, her voice echoing in her mind as the ramifications of her actions glared at her from six bloody eye sockets. She winced to stare back at them. "As grim as they look, Sharon and Dan need their bodies back to bury them."

***

The crucifixes both came down and came apart easily. The guards—under Vicky's instruction—laid the three upright bars in a row and then tied the smaller horizontal bars across them. It looked like the start of a raft. They had enough twine from taking them apart to make it work.

The three kids lay with the contours of the stretcher like thinly sliced bacon on a griddle pan. Far from level because of the crossbars, their malleable little bodies showed just how lifeless they were. It would be a while yet before rigor mortis kicked in.

None of the guards spoke as they carried the kids back. Other than the sound of the wind and the crunch of their feet through the long grass, they walked in silence. Vicky continued to stare straight ahead as she and Serj led the way at the front of the stretcher. She scanned their surroundings for signs of the diseased and Moira's army.

Scoop, Piotr, and Flynn walked behind Vicky and she heard at least two of them crying. She didn't look back to find out who. A hard lump like broken glass had balled in her own throat. She'd only just managed to stop crying; if she looked at them, it would set her off again.

After they'd passed through the solar panel field, they descended the small slope towards Home's entrance.

"So …" Serj said, "shall we show them the note?"

Vicky shrugged when the others looked at her. "Show them. They deserve to see it."

Chapter Nineteen

"So this is all *her* fault?" Dan said, the letter shaking in his hand as he glared at Vicky. "They killed *our* children to get back at her?"

What did Vicky expect? The note said why they'd done it. Ultimately, their children *had* died because of her. Had she not escaped, then Moira's community wouldn't have sought retribution. At least, that was what the letter said.

Instead of replying, Vicky looked down at the dead children on the ground in the flat grass. They'd done their best to trample it before they removed the bodies from the stretcher. She looked at the dark red holes where their eyes should have been. She looked at the cavities in their small chests. A rock of a lump rose up in her throat, but she gulped it back down. What right did she have to grieve?

Vicky drew a deep breath and looked at the gathered crowd outside of Home. Her stomach turned over and her heart fluttered to be the focus of so much rage. Would she become a pariah in the community? A Jonah that needed to be thrown overboard? At least thirty adults and as many children, they all stared at her. Given half a chance, many of them looked like they'd end her where she stood. Then she saw Stuart. The man offered her a tight-lipped smile. At least she had one person on her side.

Serj stepped towards Dan, the long grass up past his knees. "Now that's unfair," he said. "What would you have done in Vicky's situation? Would you have stayed in the community and accepted death when you had a chance to get away?"

The tension in Dan's jaw made it look like he could bite through steel. He didn't reply to Serj; instead he addressed Vicky again. "If it saved the life of my children, then yes."

Scoop—who comforted a distraught Meisha—let go of her daughter and moved forward. "Look, Dan, I know you're hurt. Of course you're hurt—"

"Let me ask *you* something, Scoop," Dan said, the wind blowing his loose-fitting shirt.

Scoop froze and looked at him.

"How would *you* feel if that—" he pointed down at the brutalised corpses of his three children "—if that was Meisha? What would you do if you saw her like that?" The June sunshine made his tear-sodden cheeks glisten.

As much as Scoop looked like she wanted to reply, she didn't. Instead, she shivered and moved close to Meisha again.

Sharon stood over her children's bodies the entire time. She clamped her hands to the bottom half of her face. While shaking her head, she rocked on the spot and muttered something to herself that Vicky couldn't understand. She then kneeled down, tore a strip from her jumper, and wiped at the eyes of her youngest. The blood had already dried against his cheeks, so she licked the makeshift cloth—zero regard for the red stain already on it—and went again at cleaning him up. No doubt she'd do the same for the other two.

The silence seemed to last an age before Dan threw his arms up in the air and addressed Scoop again. "So you have nothing to say? I *know* you'd be exactly the same as I am now, yet you expect us to accept it?"

"I'm not saying accept it," Scoop said, "but I would have done what Vicky did were I in her situation. How could she possibly think her escaping would mean Moira's community would do *this* to your children? In what world does that logic make sense?"

For the first time since coming out of Home and seeing her children, a flash of clarity ran across Sharon's otherwise washed-out features. She looked up from the ground, her long blonde hair dancing in the breeze as she spoke with an unnaturally calm tone. "All I know is we've lived in Home for close to a decade now, and we've *never* had a run-in with this community before." She levelled a stare at Vicky that cut to her core. "Now *she* comes here, and we're in a war. How many more children will die? Why don't we just give her up and be done with it?"

Piotr spoke this time. "You think that will work? You think they'll let this go now?"

But Sharon had gone again. The glaze had returned to her eyes and she shook her head at her mutilated children as an indecipherable stream of garbled nonsense issued from her mouth.

A rip opened into a chasm inside Vicky as she watched the broken mother. Although not a parent, she'd cared for a little one. She knew what it meant to fear for their safety. No one should outlive their child; it went against the natural order of things.

Movement flashed through Vicky's peripheral vision. When she spun to face it, she saw Dan had been knocked to the ground and Flynn sat on top of him. A large chunk of brick lay a few feet away from them.

Flynn raised his fist and gritted his teeth as he glared down at the man. But before he could swing for him, Vicky darted forward and put a hand on his shoulder. "Don't." She tugged on Flynn's arm and encouraged him to his feet.

Although Flynn came with her, Vicky had to pull hard to move him. Still breathing heavily, Flynn twisted away from her and continued to lean over Dan, both of his fists clenched and his face red. "Have you *seen* the community they had Vicky trapped in?"

Tears ran freely down Dan's cheeks and sobs bucked through him as he lay in the long grass. He shook his head.

"I have. They *torture* people down there. They feed them scraps of vegetable peelings and offcuts of rancid meat mixed with *used* sanitary towels."

Dan's eyes widened as he looked at Flynn.

"They have two pits down there. Did you know that?"

A shake of his head—his lips buckling out of shape—and Dan still didn't speak.

"Well, they do. One of them is a dark manhole they put people in and slide a cover over the top of. The other one is a pit filled with diseased. Of *course* Vicky escaped from that; anyone would in her situation. Your anger needs to be at Moira and her community, not at Vicky for doing what anyone else would have done." Flynn pointed at the brick on the ground. "You try a trick like that again and I'll cut your throat, you got me?"

If Dan took in what Flynn had just said to him, it didn't show. Instead, he remained on his back and brought his hands up to cover his face. He sobbed as he lay there, his quiet cries turning into full-blown screams.

"Come on," Vicky said as she tugged on Flynn's arm again.

Dan screamed louder, his broken wail calling across the open meadow.

Some of the adults in the community stayed with Sharon and Dan, but the guards walked away—the guards and Meisha. Vicky reached across and touched Flynn's back. "Thank you."

"I did it for the sake of the *community*," he said as he scowled at her. "We can't have infighting."

Although his words had been clearly designed to hurt her, Vicky couldn't rise above it. Each syllable cut to her core. Of all the people in the world, Flynn had the most direct link to her heart. She remained wide open in his presence, and he could hurt her any time he chose to.

When Vicky looked up, she found Piotr staring at her. The large man winced—like she needed his fucking sympathy. "This can't go unpunished," he said in his thick Russian accent. "We *need* to retaliate."

"We do," Vicky agreed, "but not immediately. We go down there tonight and they'll be ready for us. We need to give it a few days to wait for them to lower their guard."

Nods passed around the guards as they walked through

Home's large entryway, their footsteps echoing in the empty foyer. Moira's community would fall and Vicky would make sure her knife ended the vicious bitch.

Chapter Twenty

The moon hung as a silver fingernail in the starry sky, providing very little light and giving Vicky the perfect opportunity to hide in the darkness. Although the lack of light gave with one hand, it took away with the other. It made it much harder to navigate the uneven and tufty ground.

As Vicky walked alongside the prison in the dark, she scanned the emaciated occupants. What if she'd persuaded Aaron to trust her and he'd been thrown into the pit? What if Moira had taken some of the other prisoners too?

When Vicky saw Aaron, she let her relief out with a heavy breath. She moved close to the fence and the rich smell of dirt and shit.

Many of the prisoners looked up at Vicky's approach and saw her before Aaron did. They shuffled to meet her as she dropped her heavy bag and unzipped it. She tried her hardest to stifle her reaction to the stench as she handed out the refilled bottles of water. Home had many assets; among its best were the water filtration system and its solar power. Not many people had those luxuries in the world now.

Aaron regarded Vicky with sunken green eyes as he took a bottle of water from her. "It's been one day already. You said you'd be rescuing us within two. You coming for us tomorrow?"

Vicky looked at Aaron, his gaunt face twisted with the sneer of a skeptic. "Um …" she said.

A roll of his eyes and Aaron sighed. A lot of the others sagged around him too.

"There's been a hiccup."

"Oh, well, that's okay, then." An already sunken face, Aaron's features dropped farther. "I mean, it's not like our *lives* are on the line or anything, is it?"

The memory of the three kids flashed through Vicky's mind and she flinched at the mental image. It suddenly became harder to keep her thoughts straight. "I know that, Aaron. It's been a hard day."

"You're coming to me for therapy now?" Aaron grabbed the chain-link between them and sent a rattle along the fence when he shook it. "In case you haven't noticed, I have slightly more pressing issues to deal with. You'll have to find someone else to listen to your bullshit. Why don't you just tell us the truth?"

The others closed in like the diseased. They looked ravenous for her flesh. "Which is?" Vicky asked.

"You're not coming to rescue us."

"But we are."

The lethargy left Aaron as he surged forwards, his face crashing into the fence. "When?" he barked.

"Shh!" Vicky looked towards the section with the guards in it. "Keep it down; otherwise the answer will be never."

Although Aaron opened his mouth to reply, Vicky cut him

off, "Moira killed three of the children from the community today."

When Aaron looked like he'd say something else, Vicky added, "She gouged their eyes and hearts out. She nailed each of them to a cross."

Aaron's face dropped at the same time a gust of wind rushed through the pen. It forced the reek of rotting food and human waste at Vicky and she couldn't help screwing her nose up.

The anger left Aaron and he spoke in a soft voice. "Which three?"

"Do you know Sharon and Dan?"

"Blythe?"

Vicky looked behind her. Probably just paranoid, but it sounded like movement in the darkness. As she stared into the inky blanket of shadow, her mouth dried. She couldn't see a thing. While holding her breath, she reached down for the knife on her hip and listened for sounds of movement. Nothing. She turned back to Aaron. "Yeah, Sharon and Dan Blythe."

"All *three* of their kids?"

"Yeah."

"Fuck."

"They left a note saying they did it because I broke out. A lot of people in Home are pissed off with me."

"Fuck!" Aaron said again. "But what did they expect you to do? Stay *here*?"

"They're hurt. Their children are dead and the murderer attributed their death to me. I can't blame them for being pissed off."

A shake of his head and Aaron looked down at the ground.

"So I will get you out." Vicky looked at all of the faces on the other side of the chain-link. "I'll get *all* of you out, but this has knocked us back by a few days."

The other prisoners passed the empty water bottles back to Vicky and she put them into her bag one at a time. As she focused on loading up her pack, she said, "Your lives are important to me. I have sleepless nights thinking about you all in here. I see what you're going through, but I can't break you out on my own."

"We're three people down since you came here last," Aaron said. "Three people who'd managed to get three heads every single time they went out. This time each of them came back with two and Moira dropped them straight in the pit. No strikes, just straight in the pit."

"I promise I'll come for you soon," Vicky said.

As the last of the group slid his bottle through to Vicky, she and Aaron stared at one another. "I hope you do," he said. "I really hope you do."

***

Guilt had turned into a parasite inside Vicky. It gnawed at her, taking bigger bites with every step she took away from Aaron and the other prisoners. The previously warm summer night took on a bitter twist and Vicky shivered as she drew close to the guards' side of the complex.

Unlike the previous evening, the door to the communal building hung wide open and the firelight spilled out into the forecourt. It showed the family in the cage more clearly than when she'd last visited. Before Vicky knew it, she said, "They look like fucking ghosts."

The family only held Vicky's attention for as long as it took her to notice the woman outside the cage. The look of her sent ice through her blood. Moira.

A witch of a woman, Moira peered in at the family and the man in the cage. The flickering light from inside the communal building turned her twisted leer into a gargoyle's mask.

When Moira laughed, her wicked cackle cut through the night and all five of the prisoners jumped. So taken over with her glee, she arched her back and pushed her pelvis forward. "Someone will have to make a decision sooner or later, you know?" she said once she'd finished laughing.

Although Moira addressed the people in the cage, none of them responded. The family huddled in one corner, the mum and dad hugging the children close; the older man huddled in the other, his eyes wide as he stared at the family and shivered. It hadn't been cold enough in months for hypothermia, but the man looked to be in a bad way with something.

The crush of plastic water bottles called out as Moira slipped them through the gaps in the cage. "I'll give you guys all the water you can drink. However, to get food, you'll need to be"—she looked from the family to the man and back to the family as a wicked grin stretched across her gaunt face—"*resourceful.*"

In the silence that followed, Vicky's heart beat so hard it damn near rocked her where she stood. Each throb of her pulse kicked like a fucking horse.

Vicky's stress level peaked when the mum's shrill scream rang through the night. She stepped toward the older man in the cage. Her face twisted with rage as she jabbed her finger at him. "You'd best not touch my fucking children. I swear, if you come near us, I'll bite your fucking throat out."

The two teenage girls' eyes widened as they looked at their mum.

Moira continued to grin and bounced on the spot as if struggling to contain her excitement.

The unspoken had been pretty obvious, but something about the dad's words sank frigid dread through Vicky.

"Just so you know," he said to the man, his voice low, "you ain't eating any of us. If I were you, I'd take that idea from your head right now."

Chapter Twenty-One

Vicky kept her back to the group and looked out over the swaying grass. They were in the meadow directly outside Home, not more than fifty metres from its front door. She didn't need to watch the children being buried. Another three little ones that wouldn't inherit this shitty world. And she didn't need to be amongst the others either. Most of the people at Home still looked at her like she'd killed them herself. Besides, they needed a few of them to keep watch in case any diseased gate-crashed the funeral.

And what could Vicky say to the people of Home anyway? If she got captured and had a chance to escape again, she'd do it. A twisted bitch like Moira would always find an excuse to kill regardless of what happened around her. They needed to end her before she got to more innocent people. As long as Moira lived, she'd inflict pain.

Three other guards stood watch with Vicky. They formed a square around the congregation and took a corner each. Piotr, Flynn, and Serj all looked out over the open space.

From her position Vicky could see Piotr to her left and Flynn to her right but not Serj. He stood behind her on the opposite corner of the square. Both Piotr and Flynn's faces reflected the heavy mood. They wore deep scowls as the wind buffeted their hair and clothes while they stood ready for the diseased should they turn up.

No matter how many deep breaths or blinks, Vicky couldn't rid herself of her tiredness. Aches sat in her heavy body. Another late night from visiting Moira's community, followed by tossing and turning until it got early enough to get out of bed; it had been days since she'd had a good night's sleep. The lives of those at Home and Moira's prisoners rested so heavy on her shoulders she felt barely able to move at times. If she had the chance, she'd have to get the camouflaged family out too.

The brief flash of summer yesterday had vanished. More grey clouds clogged the sky and the wind picked up to the point where it cut to Vicky's core. Maybe it had been the grief of the past few days that had created the rock in her stomach, maybe her exhaustion caused her perpetual tremble; either way, the bitter wind certainly didn't help. In just a T-shirt and jeans, of course she'd feel it, and gooseflesh covered her arms.

Another scan of the horizon and Vicky turned to look at Scoop. She hugged a sobbing Meisha close to her. As the only one of them not on sentry duty, she gave the funeral service. Of all the guards, she was the closest to Sharon and Dan, so it seemed appropriate.

The amount of people gathered around made it impossible for Vicky to see the three children's bodies. But because she'd helped lay them down and had dug their graves, she knew Scoop was standing right by them.

"As a parent," Scoop said, her tone sombre, her eyes glazed when she looked at Sharon and Dan, "I can't imagine what you're having to go through at the moment. No one should outlive their children. I'm so sorry."

Both Sharon and Dan nodded at her before they dropped their gaze to the ground again.

"Jack, Lola, and Alvin were good kids. They were always polite, always full of energy, and always eager to help whenever they were needed. They were a credit to your wonderful parenting." Scoop's bottom lip buckled. "They shone brighter than the sun."

A lump rose in Vicky's throat and she heard some of the crowd break, the near silence punctuated with their gentle sobs.

The start of tears itched Vicky's eyeballs and she blinked repeatedly, but it did little to prevent her view of the world from blurring and her throat aching in grief.

Although Scoop spoke again, Vicky snapped out of her sadness when she turned to see an awkward form travelling towards them through the long grass. Lopsided shoulders and limp arms, the diseased woman swayed as if she were as susceptible to the breeze as the nature surrounding her. She loosed a scream that cut Scoop dead and many of the congregation looked over.

Vicky cleared the lump from her throat and shouted, "Carry on."

As the next closest guard to the diseased, Flynn stepped forward with Vicky to meet the creature.

Nearly telling him to stay back, Vicky kept it to herself. No need to humiliate the boy in front of everyone.

Vicky took off towards the diseased woman at a jog and

another one appeared over the brow of the hill beside her. The second one—a man—stood tall and slim. As she looked at him, she stopped and raised her crossbow.

Because they were downwind from the diseased, Vicky smelled their rotten stench. She shouldered her crossbow as Flynn ran past her, closed one eye to improve her aim, and pulled the trigger. The weapon kicked as she fired the bolt and a second later red mist exploded out the back of the taller one's head. His legs buckled beneath him and he went down.

Vicky loaded a second bolt and dispatched the diseased woman before Flynn could reach her. Her legs turned to jelly and she too folded to the ground.

Still five metres away, Flynn stopped, his shoulders slumped. "I *can* kill them you know."

"I know you can," Vicky replied.

"Then why waste your bolts? Why not let me take one?"

"I thought I was doing both of us a favour. They're dangerous, Flynn—"

"You think I don't know that?"

"So why fuck about? If I can take them out, then I should, right? I'm not having the blood of any more people on my hands. Especially not *yours*."

"So *now* you take responsibility?"

"I've always taken responsibility for you, Flynn."

"I'm not talking about being responsible for me. You've been *too* fucking responsible for me. I'm talking about that mess over there." Flynn looked in the direction of the pen of diseased.

Vicky lowered her voice and moved closer to him so only he could hear her. "We're doing that to protect people."

"I'm sure they'll be grateful to know that."

Vicky didn't respond.

The pair turned and walked back toward the funeral service. Both of them looked out for more diseased. When they got closer to the gathered crowd, Vicky spoke beneath her breath. "Do yourself a favour."

Flynn looked at her.

"Stop being such a jumped-up little prick."

Although he looked like he would respond, he kept it to himself. Never appropriate to kick off at a funeral, even the petulant teenager knew when to shut the fuck up.

They continued the rest of the walk back in silence and Vicky watched many people in the crowd looking up as if to check for more diseased. Although she felt Flynn's rage burning into the side of her face, she didn't give him the satisfaction of looking at him. He could keep his fury.

Closer still to the group, Vicky and Flynn split to return to their respective posts.

Although she kept her wits, Vicky turned to watch Sharon and Dan lower their children's bodies into their graves. They tossed earth on top of them. The guards had dug relatively shallow because it would have taken too long to go six feet down.

After Dan stepped back, he looked up at Vicky, tears streaming down his face, rage and accusation burning in his glare. She'd seen that look a lot lately, but it didn't hurt any less for the familiarity.

At Home Vicky felt guilty because of the dead children. Away from Home she felt guilty because of the prisoners. If she went to them when she'd promised to, she'd go tomorrow, but she couldn't do that. She wasn't ready yet. And then she had the family in the cage—the family they should have saved when they were getting door locks from Wilkinson's. The family that would have been free now had her and Serj done the right thing by them.

Vicky turned away from Dan and walked towards Home's entrance. The large door sat embedded in the steep but short hill. The service had nearly wrapped up, so she needed to get the door open for everyone; they'd be tempting fate if they stayed outside for too long.

Chapter Twenty-Two

Tuesday morning, eight a.m. Vicky never liked the meetings, and with the funeral yesterday, she nearly didn't come to this one. Now she'd arrived, she realised maybe she should have listened to her gut. As she walked up and down in front of the line of people leaning against the wall, every face stared at her like they wanted to kill her—everyone but the guards and Stuart.

Barefoot as always, Vicky paced the blue crash mats and breathed in the familiar smell of bleach. The cold rubbery surface gave way beneath her every step as the padding took her weight.

Vicky splayed her toes out as if to press every part of her foot into the soft mat. The more connected she felt to the ground, the more stable she would be in a fight. Half the people in there looked like they'd challenge her that morning.

After Sharon and Dan had made it perfectly clear who they held accountable for the death of their children, many of the other Home residents seemed to have got on-board with their way of thinking. Everything had been fine until the new girl showed up!

The screens on the canteen's wall played footage of the long-grassed meadow. A large patch had been crushed beneath the feet of the funeral goers, and three wooden crosses protruded from a mound of churned-up earth. To look at the image nearly robbed Vicky of her zeal, but she had to go on; they all had to go on.

"Aaron, from the farm," Vicky said, her raised voice carrying through the vast room.

"Jack Blythe." She looked at Sharon and Dan.

"Lola Blythe."

"Alvin Blythe."

The four names grabbed the attention of the room and Vicky let the silence hang for longer than felt natural. Just a few weeks ago she hated talking to large groups of people; now, she manipulated the silence as a skilled orator would. She held so long, half the people leaned forward in anticipation of her next words. "Moira killed the last three and still—hopefully—has Aaron imprisoned. I say hopefully because the alternatives don't bear thinking about. The barbaric community at the bottom of the hill has existed next to Home for years—"

"And we've been all right so far," Dan Blythe called out.

The guy had been through hell, so Vicky replied with as gentle a tone as she could manage. "Tell that to Aaron."

Silence ran through the place.

"If he's still alive, that is."

It hurt to make the statement. If Vicky had returned to the prisoners in the two days she'd promised them, she would have busted them out yesterday. But everything had changed when the children were killed; she had to make sure the people at

Home were ready to put a stop to Moira before she waded in. Sure, they had the pen of diseased, but if that failed, they'd have to fight.

"Imagine being dropped into a dark pit full of diseased," Vicky said. "Or being put in a hole and having decapitated heads dropped on you while you scream."

Some of the faces in the room twisted at the mention of Moira's form of torture.

"Imagine being fed pig swill covered in used sanitary towels. Imagine having such a bad stomach you shit yourself every time you sneeze. Not only that, but you have to live on hard concrete ground with no covers and twenty other people witnessing your shame. Imagine being covered in festering sores and feeling like you're going to freeze to death *every* night."

People shifted where they stood, clearly feeling discomfort at Vicky's words. And so they should.

"Imagine being laughed at, kicked, and made fun of all day, every day. Imagine being chained up and taken out to hunt the diseased for no other reason than it gives your captors pleasure."

Again, Vicky let the silence linger. The faces looked no less angry with her, but they seemed more engaged with what she had to say.

"Moira does this to people, and she's going to do it a hell of a lot more." Vicky's pulse sped. "She's going to move in on this community, and she's going to do this to *all* of you. We were training to go to war; we all knew that. I, for one, would rather be prepared"—she pointed at the wall of monitors in the canteen—"than be caught out when an army of people turn up outside. If we're going to remain safe, we have to hit them first."

A few of the faces changed. Anger gave way to the slow dawning of acceptance.

"What Moira's done to the Blythe children can*not* go unpunished."

Some people nodded.

Vicky punched her left palm with her right fist and her voice echoed in the cavernous room. "Even if I have to go on my own, I'm going to take the fight to her. I *refuse* to lie down and wait for her to come to us."

Although Vicky had more, Stuart stepped forward from the line of people. "I'll go with you."

A few seconds passed—a few long and drawn-out seconds where it looked like Vicky and Stuart would be on their own—and then Flynn stepped forward. He might be pissed off with her, but he said, "I'd follow you to hell and back, Vicky, you know that."

A wet swell of emotion bulged in Vicky's throat and she nodded as she fought to gulp it down.

Serj and Piotr, Mary, Jules, Jacob … one by one, the people of Home stepped forward and pledged to fight beside Vicky.

"This isn't about liking *me*," Vicky said while she paced in front of the people, one or two stepping forward with every passing second, "this is about protection. About making sure we're not taken over by a psychopath like Moira. About making sure she doesn't get to anyone else in this place."

When just Sharon and Dan remained pressed against the wall, Vicky walked over to them. "I'm so, so sorry for your loss. Nothing can bring your children back, I know that, but I'm going to make sure Moira pays for what she did." Pains streaked up the sides of Vicky's face from clenching her jaw, and spittle shot from her mouth. "I'll cut her eyes out and leave her heart in so she has to feel the pain for as long as her body will let her. I won't rest until she's dead, I promise you that."

Both Sharon and Dan watched Vicky. Their eyes glazed as the tears built up inside of them. First Dan, and then Sharon, nodded at Vicky's promise.

Vicky clapped her hands together and the crack of it snapped through the large room. "We go in five days' time," she said. "Ready or not, we need to take the fight to Moira's community and roll right over them."

More nods than before, the room finally seemed to be warming up to Vicky's suggestions.

"Until then, I want *everyone* preparing for war. We need to make more weapons. Spears and clubs will be best."

A wave of nods ran up and down the line.

"Any questions?" Vicky said.

Stuart raised his hand and the people around him sighed.

Vicky nearly did too, but Stuart had been the first to support her. "Yes, Stuart?"

"What if we lose?"

"We fight to win."

The least definite answer she'd ever given him and Vicky waited for his comeback. Instead, Stuart nodded and said, "Okay. I'm ready."

No one else seemed to have any questions, so Vicky said, "All of you need to rest up and get ready for this. We need to have fire in our bellies and courage in our hearts."

The crowd dispersed and the guards came over to be with

Vicky. All except Scoop, she hadn't been at the meeting either.

Before Vicky could ask the others if they'd seen her, she noticed a disturbance in the exiting crowd. A woman rushed against the tide, shoving them away as she elbowed her way through.

When Vicky made eye contact with Scoop, her heart kicked. Before she could get close, Vicky called, "What's up?"

"*Meisha*," Scoop said, and Vicky's stomach plummeted.

Wide-eyed and breathless, Scoop hissed, "She's *gone*."

Chapter Twenty-Three

Vicky stood back and looked at the space on the wall where the spare key had been, while Serj addressed Scoop. "But how long do we give it?" He stood in front of the door to Home, a new lock in his grip. "That key could fall into the wrong hands."

"Longer than a *day*." Scoop shook her head, the whites of her eyes wide in her dark face. "Jesus, Serj, you need to give Meisha longer than that."

Just the three of them there, Vicky didn't know where she stood on the argument. After all, Meisha could be dead; or worse, she could be in a cage in Moira's community. And what then? Wait until Scoop could accept that possibility, and hope Moira didn't raid them with her newly acquired key in the meantime? But then again if they didn't give her a chance to return, then they would be cutting the next generation loose. And if they did that, what the hell were they fighting for?

Vicky looked out of the large window to the left of the huge front door and watched the long grass. The sun shone brightly, making her eyes itch. At least she had good weather today. It would have been worse for Meisha to go out amongst the diseased in the rain. A heavy downpour always made it harder to hear the fuckers approaching.

A deep sigh and Serj walked close to Scoop. Holding both of her hands with his, he spoke in a soft voice. "I get where you're coming from, and were I in your situation, I wouldn't *ever* want to change the locks, but think of the worst …"

Looking back at Serj through a glazed stare, her attention shifting from one of his eyes to the other, Scoop said, "I'm *drowning* in thoughts of the worst. Whenever I let my guard down, thoughts of the worst overwhelm me."

Vicky stepped closer to Scoop and put a gentle hand against her slim lower back. "We have to protect everyone else's kids too, Scoop. If the spare key's fallen into the wrong hands …"

Scoop's shoulders slumped and she dropped her head as she stared down at the blue linoleum floor. "Can we just give her a little longer? She left a note saying she was going out to find supplies. If she's gone to the local town, she shouldn't be back yet anyway. Surely we need to give her enough time to do that?"

The appeal melted Vicky's heart. To see a fellow guard and friend in such distress … Were it Flynn, she'd demand they never change the locks. "Maybe we should give her a bit more time," she said to Serj.

Piotr and Flynn had gone to the farm to check on supplies, so the decision had to be made between Vicky and Serj.

Serj drew a deep breath before he finally shrugged and turned to Scoop. "If you remain by the door and wait for her, you can keep an eye out for anything untoward. That way, we can wait a little longer."

After she'd nodded at him, Scoop said, "Thank you." She looked at Vicky and repeated, "Thank you."

Chapter Twenty-Four

"I'll be glad when we don't have to do this anymore," Serj called after Vicky as he ran behind her toward the small but thick wooded area between them and the pen.

Vicky didn't reply. Instead, she focused on the trees up ahead, the grass whipping at her as she sprinted through it. Whenever they led a pack this way, the woods meant the difference between life and death. If they kept their wits, they could get through the space and open up enough of a lead for the final stretch.

The diseased screamed as they chased the pair. A wall of sound, it challenged Vicky's resolve and a buckle snapped through her stride.

When Vicky entered the woods, it muted their cries. For a second, the sound of her own heavy steps and ragged breaths rang out louder than the mob on their tail.

Vicky heard Serj enter the woods behind her. Despite his fitness, whenever he ran he breathed like an asthmatic in the middle of an attack.

The sound of the diseased entered a few seconds later and

their collective roar seemed to shake the trees. Vicky and Serj had picked up more of a crowd than ever before. Fuck knew how many, but when Vicky glanced back, they stretched the width of the woods.

Vicky did her best to push her panic down and searched for her route out of there. It didn't matter how many chased them, her objective remained the same—get the fuck out of the woods well before they did.

A heavy pulse and tightening lungs dragged on Vicky's progress. She pulled greedily at the pine-scented air and continued to focus in front of her, twisting and turning her way through the tightly packed space. She kept tabs on Serj by listening to his panting breaths. Apart from that, they were on their own until they got to the ropes.

When Vicky burst from the woods, the sun burned her eyes. The same happened every time and she squinted while running blind. Every footstep rolled when it landed on the uneven ground. One wrong step and she could break her ankle. If she did, she'd expect Serj to leave her behind—she wouldn't stop for him.

The few seconds of blindness seemed to last an age before Vicky's sight returned. She was now no more than fifty metres from the two ropes hanging from the tree. One for her, one for Serj.

The grass whipped at Vicky's thighs again.

When Vicky got close to the ropes, she leapt and reached out. Driven by her momentum, she grabbed the rope and swung forward over the pen of diseased. She shimmied up it while it moved.

The rope next to her swung when Serj landed on it, but Vicky didn't look across. Not yet.

Once at the top, Vicky turned to face the approaching pack. It didn't matter how many times she saw the tidal wave of insanity, whenever a horde of the fuckers chased her, cold fear wrapped her in a constrictor's grip.

Vicky's knuckles ached from how tightly she held the rope. She watched Serj climb for a second before looking at the lead diseased at the head of the pack.

The packs always had a leader, sometimes two, and that leader would always be the most adept. It ran the fastest and looked the strongest. Vicky always feared it and figured if any of them would get to her, the fucker in the lead would.

A few seconds later the alpha jumped at Vicky's rope. Not quite zero co-ordination, but not far off, the brute flailed in her general direction, hit the knot at the bottom with its face, and fell down the steep slope.

The knock from the diseased set Vicky's rope swinging again and she watched the others make even more pitiful attempts at reaching her as they fell, one by one, down the short and sharp hill leading to the holding area below.

Although she still fought for breath, Vicky found her words when she turned to Serj. "I've had enough of this now. This *has* to be the last time. We need to take these fuckers to Moira."

The diseased had all fallen into the trap now, yet Serj still looked down at them as if they could rise up and attack him from their current position. Without taking his eyes off them, he reached up and pulled the rope attached to the first gate. It swung shut with a loud *crash*.

Vicky tugged the other rope so the new arrivals could mingle with the rest of the horrible fuckers. As she looked at them, she continued to breathe heavily and said again, "This is the *last* fucking time."

Chapter Twenty-Five

After Serj had lured the diseased down to the opposite side of the pen, Vicky slid down the hill and closed the inside gate behind them. She backed off, closed the outer gate, and scrambled back up the small hill. Even with the open space and strong winds between her and the pack, their rancid stench still smothered her.

Vicky lay down on her belly and hid in the long grass so she could watch them. They had well over two hundred diseased now. Surely it had to be enough to take down Moira's community.

Serj looked over at Vicky before he pulled away from the mob. Each of them moved to the rhythm of their own torment as they watched him disappear. Some swayed from side to side, some slashed at the air as if locked in a battle with a figment of their own imaginations—if they even had imaginations anymore. Some of them bit around them as a dog would when trying to catch a fly. Despite their seeming individuality, something locked them together. They seemed to have a hive mind. It drove them and could call them all to the same cause. It could be used to get them to Moira's community.

***

"So how are we going to do this?" Serj said and Vicky jumped as he slid down next to her.

"How did I not hear you?"

Serj shrugged. "I waited."

"Huh?" Vicky said.

"I waited down there for you to come to me."

"How long have I been here?"

"Fifteen minutes at least." Serj watched the diseased too. "There's something hypnotic about them, isn't there?"

"And stupid," Vicky said. "They've watched the space you disappeared into for the entire time. You'd think one of them would have turned around by now." As if on cue, a small diseased no bigger than a six-year-old wandered through the pack. "It's never easy to see children like that, is it?"

"Poor kid," Serj said. "She looks like she's looking for her mum. Even though it's been over ten years, I still can't believe the curse that's been put on this world."

Fire burned beneath Vicky's cheeks. If they knew she'd helped release it, she'd be out of Home within seconds. Another thing the community could hate her for—and rightly so this time.

Vicky pushed the thought of Brendan to the back of her mind. The memory of the school bus in Summit City took its place. The sight of the diseased kid must have stirred it up. She thought of the splash when the glass smashed against the ground as the bus fell. The children's screams flying from the toppled vehicle. The blood.

"We need to get them to Moira's community while keeping them as far from Home as possible," Vicky said, trying to forget her memories. "You've seen how we can lead them off a ledge. We need to do that at the top of the hill and let them fall into the complex at the bottom. If this lot crash against the chain-link fence, hopefully it'll collapse."

"*Hopefully?*"

Vicky turned to look at the man. "You want guarantees from me?"

A flicker of something flashed across Serj's mahogany gaze, but he didn't say it. Maybe he did want guarantees but realised the absurdity of it. "When shall we do it, then?"

"I worry about Moira's prisoners. The sooner we get them out, the better." Two diseased scuffled for a second in front of them. They seemed unable to contain their fury, but the fight quickly died down after several slaps and a lot of growling. They both seemed to realise the futility of taking from one another what had already been taken. "I promised them we'd get them out two days ago."

"Huh?"

"Oh fuck."

"What do you mean you 'promised them'."

"Uh … I …"

"Just tell me, Vicky."

A heavy sigh and Vicky kept her attention on the diseased. "After we fitted the new locks, I went to Moira's community in the night." She winced. "Twice." Before Serj could speak, she added, "I wanted to make sure the prisoners were okay and to see how many guards we're up against."

"And?"

"I haven't been able to work that out yet. Because it was night, I assume most of them were sleeping. But if the dorms are anything to go by, then I'd say there's a *lot* of them there."

Serj scratched his head and frowned at her. "Why did you go on your own?"

"Because *you* need to look after Home."

"I'm not the only guard."

"No, but Scoop has a little girl she needs to protect and Flynn is so pissed off with me at the moment he's a fucking liability."

A look out at the horizon and Serj chewed the inside of his mouth as he seemed to consider her words.

"You remember the people we saw in town. The family," Vicky said.

"The army surplus guys?"

"Yep. Moira has them."

At first Serj's eyes widened. Then his head dropped and his shoulders sagged. "Damn."

"I know, right? She has them in a cage with a man that seems to have nothing to do with them. She's waiting until they get hungry enough to eat one another."

"*What?*"

"She wants them to turn on one another for food. There's a tense stand-off between them. At least, there was; that might have changed now." More and more of the diseased turned away from where Serj had disappeared and wandered aimlessly.

"We need to get them out," Serj said.

"Exactly. How about we attack in two days' time? I know I

told the people at Home five, but if they don't have to fight, then we'll save lives, right? Hopefully we can get it all sorted before they even have to think about it. Also, the longer we wait, the more likely it is the prisoners will be gone when we get there."

A deep sigh and Serj continued to watch the diseased in the pen.

Before he could reply, Vicky gasped and her stomach flipped. "Oh my *god*." She pointed down at the pack.

Only aware of him in her peripheral vision, Vicky noticed Serj turn to look where she indicated. "Oh fuck," he said. "It's …"

"Meisha," Vicky finished for him.

The sound of the wind filled the silence between them before Serj said, "How the fuck are we going to tell Scoop?"

Chapter Twenty-Six

When they reached Home's entrance, Vicky pulled her key out and cast a glance around her one last time. The area seemed clear, the grass moving as she would expect it to in the wind. She focused on the keyhole and unlocked the door.

The second Vicky stepped inside, she found Scoop waiting in the foyer. Heavy bags sat beneath her bloodshot eyes.

"Have you seen Meisha?" she said.

Vicky shook her head. "No. Sorry." She and Serj looked at one another as he followed her into the foyer.

They'd discussed it on the way back and decided it would serve no purpose to tell Scoop about Meisha. The girl had gone, driven away by the disease. Sure, Scoop would need closure, and she could have that after they'd set the diseased loose on Moira's community. It had taken them months to fill the pen, if Scoop knew about Meisha now, she'd want to get her back and bury her. Who wouldn't, right? But that couldn't happen. To try to get Meisha from the pen could jeopardise everything. Meisha couldn't be saved, but Home still could.

The look in Scoop's eyes took on a sound in Vicky's mind.

To watch her fellow guard—her irises shifting from side to side—made her think of a great structure cracking as it fell. A tower as tall as Pisa giving way at the bottom, creaking and groaning until the entire thing came crashing down.

Although Vicky reached out to hold Scoop's hands, Scoop either didn't notice or didn't care because she completely disregarded the gesture. Maybe she sensed the betrayal.

Silence in the foyer save for the click of the lock as Serj closed the door. Vicky watched Scoop's eyes glaze as if she'd retreated into her own mind. Scoop then turned around and walked away down the stairs, clearly in shock as she moved on autopilot.

A look across at Serj as she drew a deep breath and Vicky exhaled hard, her cheeks puffing out with the action. They'd done it for the right reasons. The uninfected needed to be the priority, regardless of how hard she'd just found it to lie to her friend.

Chapter Twenty-Seven

The half-moon hung in the near cloudless sky. Brighter than the last time Vicky had visited, it ran white highlights along the wire of the chain-link fence. It showed the prisoners beyond, their eyes sunk so deep in their gaunt faces they appeared to have no eyes at all.

The moonlight made it easier for Vicky to navigate the rough ground but still gave her enough shadow to hide in. Although, she took no comfort from it and her stomach clamped tight with anxiety. Regardless of the cloaking darkness, it would only take a torch to reveal her in plain sight. But she had to keep going. They were finally going to move on Moira's community and the prisoners needed to know.

Aaron looked like shit. Worse than before. His skin clung to his face as thin as a layer of film. To look at him reminded Vicky of the Gothic paintings she'd seen of skulls on writing desks. The source of light always came from a melting candle off to one side and cast appropriately eerie shadows. Fuck knew which museum she'd seen them in; the Tate, the National Gallery … a lot of years had passed since then and it hardly mattered now anyway.

Exhaustion clearly gripped Aaron, who slowly turned his head to Vicky when she stepped forward. Before he spoke, he heaved a weary sigh, the inhale lifting his entire body. "How long?"

"Two days." Vicky dumped her heavy bag and went through the routine of passing water and food to Aaron first and then the other prisoners.

"Two *days*! What the fuck, Vicky? You said that three days ago!"

"I'm sorry."

"Well, *that's* okay then." Laboured breaths ran through him as he lay against the fence and stared at her through listless eyes.

"I can see how it looks, but we have problems to deal with at Home." Vicky gave some carrots to the people who lined up for them and already took some of the empty water bottles back.

"One of the guards' kids has gone missing. It's causing a lot of disruption. I promise I'll be back in two days. I won't let anything stand in the way of it." Vicky checked behind her for the diseased and touched the knife at the back of her trousers. Up until now she'd worn the blade on her hip and taken it off inside Home. But with the amount of animosity around her at the moment, she'd decided to conceal the weapon on her at all times.

"For what good your promise is!" Aaron said. "Two more people went in the pit today, you know?"

Vicky didn't reply.

"*And* they brought back three heads from the hunt! Moira's punishing people for fun now. I've managed to meet the quota for heads every day, which apparently means fuck all. And I don't know how much longer I can keep it up for." Several hungry gulps of air and he added, "I'll be in the pit soon."

"Just be prepared, okay? Be ready to bust out. We have enough diseased penned up to tear through this place. It'll be your best chance to run. Just before it happens, I'll bring some hammers down. When there's chaos outside, you'll be able to smash up the concrete ground and lift the fence up."

"Why don't you bring us the hammers now?"

"Because Moira will find them. It'll ruin your chances of escape and our chance to surprise her."

Before either of them could say anything else, Moira's shriek cut through the night. At first Vicky thought it came from a diseased and spun around, drawing her knife. What she'd give for her crossbow right now. She'd left it behind because she needed to carry supplies on her back. Not ideal, but she probably wouldn't hit much in the dark anyway.

Then it came again. "Yes! Yes! Yes!"

After sharing a look with Aaron, Vicky threw frantic gestures at the people in the cage—hurry the fuck up with the water bottles and pass them back. A shake took a hold of her in her haste to pack her bag, the empty bottles crunching as she threw them in. Fortunately Moira seemed too occupied at that moment to notice anything else.

The zip on Vicky's bag creaked through the night air and she turned to Aaron again. "Hang on in there. I promise I'll get you free." She then darted into what shadow she could use and moved alongside the prison until she came to the guards' section of Moira's complex.

Like the last time she'd visited the community, the door to

the guards' communal area hung wide open. Firelight rippled across the forecourt. It lit up the cage, twisting and bending the shadows on the bars as if manipulating the metal itself.

Vicky found a bush on an elevated mound. It gave her both something to hide behind and a view into the forecourt beyond.

The mum of the family shouted at the man in the cage. "I said stop looking at my girls. I don't know what you want from them, but it won't happen."

Moira stood close to the bars, her eyes wild in her craggy face, her crazy black hair bouncing as she hopped on the spot.

No more than a defensive ball, the man recoiled in the cage from the mother's wrath. He raised his shaking hands above his head and looked at the ground in total subservience. "Please, I don't plan on doing anything. I don't mean you any harm. Please."

"He's lying, Simon," the mum said to the man in the cage with her, and she pointed down at the cowering wreck again. "I can see it in his face."

If anyone had insanity in their face at that moment, it didn't come from the older man. Moira maybe, the mum for sure, and even Simon seemed to be catching the crazy bug, his wide eyes bulging in his gaunt face.

Simon moved next to his wife and grew more animated, the situation clearly pumping him up. "Are you calling my wife a liar?"

Vicky jumped to see the mum of the family dart forward and drive a hard kick into the man's face. It connected with a loud *clop* before the dad piled in after her. They went to work on the older man, a flurry of punches and kicks moving in the dancing light.

When the dad raised his fist, Vicky noticed the glisten of blood on it. His or the man's, she couldn't tell, but only one side fought the battle. While being attacked, the older man curled up and covered his face.

Spittle flew from the mother's mouth when she leaned over him, her teeth bared. "You won't win this. This is the fucking end for you."

Until that point, Vicky had focused on the mum and dad. Although when she looked at the two girls behind them, her heart sank. They hadn't been taken over with the rage infecting their parents. Instead, they stood at the back of the cage—seemingly pressing themselves as hard against the bars as they could—and they hugged one another. Both of them cried freely.

But Vicky didn't watch them for long.

When the mum dropped to her knees next to the man, Vicky shuddered to see her wild face. The firelight glistened on her teeth when she opened her mouth wide and dived in on the cowering man's neck.

The man screamed, Moira cackled, the guards cheered, the girls cried, the dad continued to beat the shit out of the man, and the mum pulled away, blood dribbling down her chin and neck as she chewed on the liberated piece of flesh that had been a part of the man only moments before.

Knots clamped Vicky's guts tight and a nauseating fire burned in her belly. Whatever else she did in this life, she would take Moira down.

Chapter Twenty-Eight

Maybe it would have been a good time for Vicky to leave. The guards and Moira all watched the barbaric attack in the cage and it gave her the perfect opportunity to move from shadow to shadow until she got out of there. But she didn't. Instead, she stayed and watched events unfold in front of her, her stomach tense and her jaw slack.

The mum's eyes rolled as if she were about to vomit, yet she continued to chew the man's flesh. When she gulped it down, Vicky's stomach flipped.

The mum looked at the others, a goatee of blood dribbling from her chin.

Even Moira's laugh died down at that point. "You fucking sicko," she said.

Some form of realisation sank through the mum's features and her mouth fell half open. Only moments earlier she'd been lost in the frenzy of the kill, but in the face of Moira's berating, she seemed to be coming back.

"How the fuck do you do that to another human being?" Moira said.

Despite being over twenty metres away and seeing everything in the poor light of the fire, Vicky noticed the shake running through the mum.

The mum looked from the dead man down to her blood-covered hands and then up to her family. Even her husband backed away from her, her daughters still pushing against the bars as if their applied pressure would get them out of there.

The frantic cycle repeated several times before the mum focused on Moira. "What have I done?"

The accusation of a few seconds ago left Moira's frame and she spoke with a soft voice. "You've just killed a man, dear. And you've eaten some of him." Her tone stiffened and she shouted, "Isn't that fucking obvious?"

As the mum shook her head and rocked back and forth, Moira's cackling laugh returned and rang out into the night. The shrill punch of glee startled a rabbit next to Vicky, which exploded to life and ran away from the bush. By the time it had vanished from sight, Vicky had only just drawn her knife. Were that a diseased, it would be eating her face off by now.

Moira continued to goad the mum. "You've just bitten into him like he's a cooked ham." She used her long and bony index finger on her right hand to jab at her temple as she laughed louder. "You're fucking *mental*."

When the mum looked at her partner and her girls, she shook more violently. As if a hypothermic seizure came over her, she jittered uncontrollably, the man's blood still running from her face.

Not that her clear distress stopped Moira. "I can't believe you thought you had to eat him. What the fuck's wrong with you? I was planning on letting you out today too."

The brief moment of lucidity seemed to pass for the mum, who repeatedly shook her head as she walked in small circles inside the cage. She spread the fingers on both of her hands out and stretched them back as if locked in a spasm. She clapped her palms together, seemingly trying to avoid the fingers connecting with one another.

The girls remained at the back of the cage and clung together as if they could keep each other afloat in the choppy sea of insanity. They stared at their mother, or what used to be their mother.

Moira sneered as she looked at the family and shook her head. She then turned to her guards. "Get them out."

After one guard opened the cage, four of them moved in and grabbed a family member each. The family came without resistance, all of them looking down at the recently dead man as they passed him.

Chapter Twenty-Nine

More guards joined the ones who'd dragged the family out until there were thirteen in total surrounding them. They followed Moira around the side of the complex where the prisoners were. Vicky moved over with them, staying in the shadows to remain hidden.

"*No*," the dad said, his call running out into the night. "Don't lock us up *again*."

Vicky hadn't noticed the dad's bare feet until one of the guards stamped on them and he screamed. Another guard punched him on the chin, rocking him to the point where the one leading him had to hold him up.

A quick check over both shoulders and Vicky couldn't see any diseased. They might be there, but if they hadn't been attracted to the sound, then maybe she'd be okay.

The dad had asked Moira not to lock him up again. Vicky had no doubt the crazy bitch would oblige him.

When Moira walked toward the two manhole covers, Vicky dropped her head and sighed.

At the cover over the pit of diseased, Moira stopped to look up at one of her guards. She then pointed down at it.

"No," Vicky whispered. "Don't do it."

Backflips turned through Vicky's stomach as she watched on and listened to the scratch of the metal manhole cover against the concrete surrounding it. When she looked at the cage of prisoners, she saw Aaron watching her. Maybe he couldn't see her. Maybe he just guessed she was still there. Either way, she stepped back a few paces into a darker spot.

Something close to hope burned in Vicky's chest as she watched Moira and her guards. Maybe the hideous matriarch just wanted to taunt the family. Hopefully, she'd change her mind and throw them in with the other prisoners.

The sharp tear of gaffer tape echoed in the open space as one of the guards pulled off a long strip and wrapped it around the mouth of the youngest of the two girls. He then used more to pin her arms to her body. When the guard had finished, the silver tape sheathed and gagged the girl. It left her standing pencil straight.

An evil grin lit the guard's face as he pulled out another length of tape no more than about twenty centimetres long. He bit it free and pressed it over the girl's nose. He laughed as he pinched it and the girl's eyes spread wide from where she clearly couldn't breathe.

The girl's cheeks puffed out in panic and she shook her head. She tried to say something, but it came out as no more than a muffle. Her pale skin turned red. Tears ran down her cheeks.

The dad broke free and ran for his daughter. Before he could get to her, another guard drove the end of a baseball bat into his stomach. It forced a loud *oof* from the dad, who folded to his knees on the ground.

Most of it didn't seem to register with the mum, who stared into space and looked catatonic while the eldest of the two girls cried and stared at the ground.

Suddenly, as if their situation had only just dawned on her, the mum broke out into hysterical screams. The guard who'd just dropped the dad let his bat fall and drove a hard cross into the mum's chin, but she remained on her feet.

When the mum drew a breath as if to scream again, the guard raised a fist at her and grimaced.

The mum stopped.

A slightly smaller guard than the one who'd attacked the mum lifted the youngest girl and waddled over to the open manhole with her as if she were no more than a fence post. With little ceremony, he held her over the wide hole and dropped her.

Vicky heard nothing of the girl's passing other than the scream below from the frenzied diseased. Like Meisha, Jack, Lola, and Alvin, she wouldn't see the future of this fucked-up world.

The dad looked like he tried to call out again, but he fought to breathe from the bat's winding and didn't seem to have it in him. So when he jumped to his feet, it startled Vicky. Two steps towards Moira and another guard clotheslined him.

The dad hit the ground flat on his back and the guard who'd taken him down leaned over him and punched him square in the face. The dad fell limp.

No need for gaffer tape, they dropped the dad in next.

Both the older daughter and the mum shook and cried. At least they'd learned to keep their mouths shut, for what good it would do them.

For the next few minutes, Vicky tasted the bile of indigestion as she watched the guards wrap the mum and daughter in gaffer tape like they'd done to the youngest girl.

They carried them to the manhole and dropped them in one after the other. They might have twisted and writhed against their captor's grip on the way over, but it didn't matter; they stood no chance of escaping.

***

After just a few seconds, the sound of the diseased's frenzy vanished and gave way to the wet ripping sounds of tearing flesh.

A click of fingers from Moira and one of the guards—a short and slim woman with the body of a young boy—slid the manhole cover back across. It muffled the sound of the feasting diseased, which made it easier for Vicky to hear the vicious woman address her guards. "I've had enough of this bullshit. We need to get ready to go to war with Home. I want that place for my own."

A cold chill seeped through Vicky's veins and the desire to run back to Home coiled within her, but she had to wait. Any movement and they'd see her now they had nothing else to focus on.

Vicky remained crouched in the bushes—her bent legs cramped from her awkward position—and she watched the guards slowly move away from the scene. They took their time as they headed back to the other side of the complex.

One final glance at Aaron and the gaunt man raised his eyebrows. Vicky stared back for what felt like the longest time before she dipped a nod. They'd get them out of there whether he believed it or not.

Chapter Thirty

Slightly out of it from another active night and the memory of the family at Moira's community, Vicky raised her hand, rocked on her feet as if her legs could give way at any moment, and stared at the group through slightly out of focus eyes. She hadn't slept well for days and every sluggish movement felt just at the edge of her co-ordination.

Even Flynn raised his hand. In what seemed to be a constant mission to challenge Vicky, even he could see the logic in what they proposed. Fed up with being the villain, Vicky relaxed as she watched Serj finally be a leader.

The five guards stood in the bleached stink of Home's foyer. Four of them had their hands in the air. Scoop didn't. When she'd seen the hands go up, she did what she'd done since Tuesday morning when Meisha vanished; she looked out of one of the large windows of Home and stared at the tall and swaying grass as if her daughter would emerge from it. But the diseased didn't heal and she wouldn't be getting out of the pen until someone let her out.

To Vicky and Serj, Meisha had to be treated as a number.

They couldn't jeopardise their plan of setting the pack on Moira's community. They had to make this decision with their heads. The war with Moira had to end before anyone else died, and they had to strike before Moira hit them. Because Vicky had woken up to this meeting, she hadn't had a chance to talk to Serj about what she'd seen the night before and tell him they needed to release the diseased now.

The guards lowered their hands and Serj walked across to Scoop. The only sound in the space came from the gentle pad of his feet over the blue linoleum floor. He placed a hand on Scoop's shoulder and looked into her eyes. "I'm so sorry, but it's four to one. It's been a couple of days now. Meisha should be back."

Scoop's breakfast—fresh made bread and a vegetable broth—sat on the floor by her feet, picked at but largely untouched. Vicky had instructed the kids in the community to bring Scoop regular meals, which they'd done since Tuesday morning. Not that getting a meal to her friend three times a day covered up the toxic guilt eating away at her. One sentence, 'Your daughter is five hundred metres away and she's one of them', would end her search, but they couldn't tell her that.

Scoop opened her mouth to reply, but Serj cut her off, his tone sharp. "What would *you* do in our situation?"

Vicky recognised the guilt in Serj's defensive response, but when she looked at Flynn, Piotr, and Scoop, she saw the slightly shocked expressions in reaction to his outburst. A usually calm man, it certainly seemed out of character.

After Scoop closed her mouth, her dark eyes welling up, Vicky walked over and hugged her tightly. She opened her heart as much as she could and breathed through her mouth because of the woman's smell. It reminded her of a dirty dog, but who could tell her to shower with things as they were?

For the entire time Vicky hugged her, Scoop locked up tight and stared out of the large window into the long and grassy field, rigid as she stood pole straight.

When Vicky pulled away, the woman she called a friend stared at her like she wanted to set fire to the world with her in it. Like she knew something was amiss.

The June sun shone through the huge window and heated the foyer. Sweat lifted beneath Vicky's clothes, so she stepped back a pace.

Tension wound the air tight before Serj said, "We'll give her one more day and then we're changing the locks, okay?"

Not gratitude, but a slight weakening of her jaw and Scoop nodded at the other four guards, sat down on the floor again, and turned to look out of the window.

***

A few minutes passed where none of the guards spoke as they all watched Scoop on the floor. The chatter from the canteen came up the stairs and filled the space.

If only the rest of the guards would just fuck off, Vicky could talk to Serj about what Moira had said. They needed to act before the crazy bitch could attack them. They also needed to step up the security in Home; they couldn't have Moira catching them unawares.

Vicky eventually cleared her throat, the sound of it echoing in the hard space. "Guys, we need to get people in the monitor room so we can watch Home's perimeter during the day. It'll be useless at night because we won't see anything."

Not that Vicky had said it directly, but Scoop looked over at her, her face streaked with tears. "I ain't moving from this spot. I need to be next to this door when my little girl returns. You know what? Change the locks if you need to; I ain't moving until she comes back anyway."

"Flynn, you need to do the first shift," Vicky said because she had no reply for Scoop. They'd get her in the monitor room when they needed to. After all, it gave her a better view of the outside than just looking through the window.

Flynn turned toward Vicky, instantly on the aggressive as he screwed his face up. "What the fuck?"

Despite the rise in her heart rate, Vicky forced calm through her words. "What's with the attitude?"

"What do you think? You're *always* trying to lock me up in places. Or chain me to a desk outside the gym. Anything as long as I can't get hurt. Fucking hell, Vicky, you won't even let me fight the diseased if you can avoid it. What the fuck was that about at the funeral? You put your own life in danger to stop me having to fight a diseased. You've *seen* me kill them plenty of times already."

A look at Serj and Vicky returned her focus to Flynn. She couldn't deny he had a point, but she'd take his wrath over his death all day long. "We're going to take turns, Flynn."

Flynn continued to glare at Vicky, his boyish face locked tight.

In her peripheral vision, Vicky felt Piotr watching her, but she didn't look over. Instead, she drew a deep and steadying breath and said, "I'll draw up a rota. You first, and then we'll break the day up into two-hour shifts so it doesn't get too boring."

Flynn still glared at her.

Sure, Flynn had a point, Vicky did want to protect him, but at that moment, she thought more about Moira. They needed the earliest possible warning of her impending attack. But to tell Flynn that would be to admit what she'd been doing in the evenings. If the others knew, they'd also know they needed to set the diseased free. They wouldn't let just Vicky and Serj do it. Scoop would see Meisha, and Flynn would be out there with hundreds of diseased. Although the boy could handle himself, Scoop couldn't see Meisha. It would fuck everything up.

Piotr put an arm around Flynn. "Come on, mate, we all need to put a shift in."

After he'd looked at Piotr, Flynn scowled at Vicky again. "Someone best come and get me in two hours." Without another word, he spun around and walked off down the stairs into the canteen in the direction of the monitor room.

Vicky sighed as she watched him go. At least after they attacked Moira's community, she wouldn't have to lie to them anymore. She'd be stepping down from her role too. Let someone else make decisions for the good of the group. She didn't need the burden of it.

Chapter Thirty-One

A few minutes had passed since Flynn left the foyer for the monitor room. Piotr, Scoop, Vicky, and Serj stood in the near silence and stared out of the windows to the meadow beyond. The sounds from the canteen continued to come up at them, but other than that, Vicky heard nothing. It seemed like they all remained beside Scoop to support her as she waited for Meisha, for whatever good that would do. In truth, Vicky waited because she needed Serj on his own. She needed to tell him about her visit to Moira's community the previous night.

"I'm going to get some breakfast," Serj finally said. "Can I get you anything, Scoop?"

None of the others spoke as they waited for Scoop to reply. When she didn't, Serj said, "I'll catch up with you guys later, then."

To watch him walk away made Vicky want to call after the man—but the others, or Piotr at least—would want to know what she had to say. A couple of seconds after Serj had left, she turned to the tall Russian. "I'll see you later, yeah?" she said, and before he could reply, she'd already run off after Serj.

Vicky caught up with Serj at the bottom of the stairs and walked next to him. Many of Home's residents seemed to be in the canteen, having breakfast. She spoke from the side of her mouth so they wouldn't hear. "I need to talk to you."

Before Serj could reply, Sharon and Dan Blythe stepped in front of the pair. They both looked like shit as they glared at Vicky through drawn and exhausted faces. It wouldn't be long before she found one of them in her room with a knife in their hand.

A look from the bereaved parents and back to Serj again and Vicky shook her head. "Don't worry about it. I'll catch you later."

As Vicky walked away, her mind ran in circles. They needed to act soon. They needed to set the diseased loose on Moira's community before it was too late. They needed to make sure no one found out about Meisha.

Chapter Thirty-Two

Vicky opened her eyes, her head thick from sleep. A second later, clarity rushed through her mind with a kick of adrenaline and she sat bolt upright. After weeks of insomnia, why had she fallen asleep today? "Fuck!"

When Vicky stood up on her weak legs, she wobbled and had to rest against the cold wall of her bedroom. At least it only had one bed in it now. The dexterity required to go from asleep to shuffling along between the two beds a second later would have been too much for her. A glance down and she saw her shoes remained on her feet.

By the time Vicky had stepped out into the corridor and closed the door behind her, she moved more easily. After a few paces, she picked up her speed and walked with a fast march towards the canteen. Because very few watches worked, the screens in the canteen were now the only place she could get an accurate reading of the time. It could be the middle of the day, it could be evening already; because there were no windows in Home, she needed to see the monitors to know.

As much as she wanted to sprint to the canteen, Vicky didn't need to attract unwanted attention. Instead, she kept at a fast walk. Her footsteps echoed in the enclosed space of the corridor as she strode down it.

When Vicky entered the large communal area at the end, she looked at the monitors on the wall. An exasperated sigh and she muttered, "Fuck," again. The sky had turned dark blue, the thick grass almost black because of the encroaching darkness. The clock on the screen showed a digital reading of the time: 8:31p.m.

The canteen sat relatively empty. Dinner had finished. A scan around the place and Vicky couldn't see Serj anywhere. Although she did see Flynn at a table by himself. When he looked up, she pulled a tight-lipped smile at him and went over.

As she got close, Flynn glared at her from behind a dark scowl. No time for drama, she cut to the chase. "Have you seen Serj?"

"He's in the monitor room. I thought you'd know that with it being *your* idea and all."

Vicky ignored the crack in his tone and looked back at the screens on the wall as if her attention would somehow make time move slower.

"And you'll be pleased to hear he's changed the locks," Flynn added. "So you've got your way with that too."

"But you voted for that as ..." Vicky stopped herself. She didn't have time for this. "You know what? Never mind. I moved you out of my room so you could grow."

Flynn laughed.

"What?" Vicky said.

"You say that, but you stop me growing every chance you

get. If it came from a nurturing and motherly place, maybe it would be easier to take. But it doesn't. You either totally blank me or you disempower me in front of everyone by stopping me fighting the diseased. You want me to be a guard, but you won't let me guard. You're a fucking control freak."

As much as Vicky wanted to argue back, she didn't. He had a point and she didn't have time. It seemed like every glance at the screens showed a rapidly darkening world outside. "You're right, and I'm sorry. I'm trying to do the best by you and I'm clearly getting it wrong. I've had a lot on my plate lately and I'm not being very level-headed about things at the moment."

"We're supposed to help each other as guards," Flynn said.

Vicky didn't respond and looked back at the monitors: 8:32.

"So let us help you," Flynn continued. "You've been acting strange. I know you're probably doing something for the greater good of the community, but you're pushing everyone away while you're doing it. I think I understand you, but a lot of the people here don't. To them, you're just a heartless bitch that can make the tough decisions without any apparent remorse. I love you, Vicky, but you need to let me in some more."

The words caught Vicky off guard and she momentarily froze. Tears itched her eyeballs, but she blinked them away. How did a teenage boy have a better grasp on life than her? For the past decade or so she'd been so focused on making sure shit got done, she'd failed to do anything about the relationships in her life. It had been easy for her to take people for granted when circumstances had forced them together. She never had to admit to caring. Another several blinks and she said, "I *will* talk to you."

Accusation sat on Flynn's chiseled face and his tone had an aggressive spike to it. "Go on, then."

Another glance at the monitor on the wall: 8:33. "But I can't now. I'm sorry."

By the time Flynn tutted at her, Vicky had already spun on her heel and headed in the direction of Serj and the monitor room.

Chapter Thirty-Three

It took no more than a couple of minutes to get to the monitor room, but it already felt like too long. Vicky slammed the handle on the door down and entered without knocking. The second she walked in, Serj spun around in his chair and looked up at her, shock in his wide eyes at the sudden intrusion.

"Vicky?"

"We've got to get out *now*."

Confusion crushed Serj's heavy features. "What are you talking about?"

Vicky looked at the ever-darkening images on the monitors, her chest tightening with panic. "Moira's going to attack us."

"When?"

"Soon. I went there last night."

"*Again?*"

"I watched her kill the family dressed in camouflage. The mum lost the plot, kicked the shit out of the guy in the cage with them, and then ate a chunk from his neck."

"What the fuck?"

"I know, right? She'd gone off the edge by that point. Properly fucking lost it. Anyway, after that, Moira called her crazy and dropped the entire family in the pit with the diseased in it."

"And what's this got to do with her attacking us?"

The monitors and large computers raised the temperature of the room. Sweat lifted on Vicky's brow from her rush over there, which she wiped away with the back of her sleeve. "After she'd dropped the family in, she said they need to attack us soon. That she's going to take Home for her own." A tightness ran through Vicky's chest. So stressed she felt her panic spilling over.

"So why are you only telling me this now?"

"I fell asleep."

"You *what*?"

"Look, don't judge me. I haven't slept for days. It was the only time I haven't wanted to fall asleep and I sparked the second I lay down. I couldn't help it."

"Shit!"

"Right? We need to set the diseased loose on them."

A look at the monitors and Serj turned back to Vicky. "But it's getting late and I have another fifteen minutes in here."

"Yeah, but no one's taking over after you because it's too dark to see anything, so what does it matter if we leave a little early? No one will know." Before Serj could respond, Vicky said, "Look, I know it's getting rapidly darker outside, but we *have* to try. The longer we leave this, the more likely Moira is to attack us."

"Why don't we just tell the others?"

Vicky put her hands on her hips and tilted her head to one side at him.

"Meisha," Serj said. "Fuck."

"Exactly." Vicky shook her head. "If Scoop sees her daughter and the others find out we've been hiding this from her … They weren't happy about the pen in the first place, this will only prove how bad an idea it was. We need to go out, plan the route to Moira's community, and lead the diseased over there before dark."

Another look at the monitors, but Serj didn't respond until he said, "How will we get past Scoop on the door?"

"She has to use the toilet once in a while."

"Right," Serj said. "Let's go, then."

Chapter Thirty-Four

The canteen didn't have many people left in it. Some of the adults remained up playing bridge and other card games, but all the children had left, and most importantly, Vicky couldn't see Piotr or Flynn.

Every second in the place took a second of daylight away from them, and they'd been sat there waiting for the past twenty minutes already.

"What if she's only just been to the toilet?" Serj asked as he frowned at the screens: 9:12 p.m.

Vicky scratched her head and checked the contents of her bag. She'd stopped at the weapons room and put three hammers in there for the prisoners. Small enough to get through the gaps in the fence, and hopefully they'd break up the concrete for them. "Hopefully she hasn't, but if we have to wait too long, then I suppose we don't go out tonight. All we can do is wait and see if Scoop moves. We can't force it."

Vicky looked at the short stairs leading to Home's foyer and she saw Scoop emerge as if on cue. The woman looked delirious as she walked, so exhausted from very little sleep she didn't even notice Vicky and Serj watching her.

Once she'd left the canteen in the direction of the toilets, Vicky looked at Serj and nodded. "You ready?"

"As I'll ever be. Oh, wait," he said, pulled a key on a shoelace from his pocket and held it out to her. "This is for the new lock. Just in case only one of us makes it back."

Although Vicky took it, she shook her head. "Don't be soft. Come on, let's go."

They both got to their feet and headed for Home's entrance.

Chapter Thirty-Five

Vicky walked quickly alongside the pen, with Serj next to her, their backs to the river as they headed in the direction of Moira's community. The jog over there and now their fast march made her sweat. The hammers in her backpack sometimes shifted to awkward angles and jabbed into her spine. Despite it getting darker, the heat of summer remained in the air.

They walked along the side of the pen farthest from Home. Vicky had never been on this side before. The grass came up to just below her breasts and dragged on her progress. Not great considering the rapidly dwindling light, but they needed to tread the route they'd lead the diseased on before they tried to run it with over two hundred of the fuckers on their backs.

The groans and moans followed them as they walked, the rotten stench snaking up Vicky's nostrils. Whenever she glanced across, she saw Meisha. Even a cursory look into the pack and the girl's tormented face stared back at her. One of the most well-balanced teenagers she'd ever met, Meisha had had her shit together. Scoop had been a good mother and loved her dearly. Meisha had worn it well.

It made it harder for Vicky to see the diseased as monsters when familiarity stared back at her. Innocence and purity ravaged by the hideous plague she'd helped loose on the world.

Not only did she look at the girl—her dark skin turning blacker from where she'd already started to rot—but she looked at the fat dude next to her. A lumberjack shirt and beard, he looked to be in his mid-forties. Probably a dad before all this happened. Someone who loved his family, his beer, and his day of sports on television on a Sunday. Just an average Joe. Another person unfairly turned because Vicky had helped set the virus free.

An old woman stood next to the man. She looked to be at least seventy years old. If anything, the disease seemed to have injected a new lease of life into her. She might have had the rambling and twitchy gait of the inflicted, but the way she bobbed and weaved as if trying to dance her way free of the disease spoke of someone decades younger than her. "Hardly a fucking cure for arthritis though, is it?"

"Huh?" Serj said as he looked across.

Vicky shook her head. "Nothing." Before Serj could say anything else, she picked the pace up a little. If they ran now, they'd have no running left when they needed it most, so she kept at a fast walk. "So if we lead them around this way when we let them out, it'll keep them as far away from Home as possible."

"Makes sense," Serj replied, looking around at their overgrown surroundings. "I just hope we don't have to run too fast. I'm still not confident we can get this done before dark."

"It'll be fine," Vicky said and sped up some more. "They'll

be slowed down by the grass as much as we'll be."

Worry lines creased Serj's face. "But can they see in the dark better than us?"

"Have you *seen* their eyes?"

Serj didn't respond and rightly so because Vicky didn't have a clue if they could see in the dark or not. They should be tripping over their own feet, but they weren't.

In all the time they'd contained the diseased, the thick fences had held. Because of that, Vicky didn't think about the creatures as much as she maybe should have. When she looked at them all reaching out to her, she shook her head. Never good to get complacent around the fuckers. She looked across again. They snarled and hissed, biting the air and moaning as if it caused them physical pain to be restrained.

The tree with the ropes hanging down from it marked the edge of the pen. As they passed it, Vicky looked out over the dark sky and sighed. "I hope we never have to lure any more of them here again. I'll be glad when we finally put our plan into action."

Serj nodded. "Me too."

***

Vicky led Serj to the top of the hill looking down on Moira's community and inhaled a lungful of the fresh night. The light had got to the point where it became almost tangible. The dark blue fuzz of those moments between day and night had thickened the air around them.

They'd come to a different point on the hill than usual, one further from Home. "We should be able to lead them off this bit."

The wind picked up, and when Vicky looked at Serj, she saw him pull his hair from his brow and hold it there as he nodded in response to her. His eyes were narrowed to slits, probably from a combination of both the sharp wind and the lack of light.

To look down at Moira's community—a chicken coop for people—lifted nausea up through Vicky's stomach and dragged a bitter taste into her mouth. "How can someone be as cruel as her? What the fuck do they achieve? Just to think of the prisoners she keeps down there … I hope Aaron's okay."

It took for Vicky to look at Serj again before he replied. A shake of his head and he said, "It's fucking tragic. When you take away the rules, some people feel the need to let out their darker side. I wonder what happened to her before this and why she feels the need to be such a cunt to everyone?"

Before Vicky could reply, he added, "I don't know if we'll have the light for this tonight, Vick. Especially if we need to get the hammers to the prisoners before we set the diseased free."

Vicky opened her mouth to respond, but the words caught in her throat when she heard the sound of voices nearby.

Serj tugged on Vicky's arm and dragged her behind a large bush close to them.

Vicky peered through the gaps to see the silhouettes of people appear. The gang numbered eight in total. They had to be Moira's people.

Careful to avoid them, both Vicky and Serj moved around the outside of the bush to remain out of the gang's way as they walked past it. Although she didn't want to use it, Vicky kept her sweating palm wrapped around the handle of the knife in the back of her belt just in case. She held her breath as she watched them.

One of the men said, "So if we go over there tomorrow and kick the front door in, we should be able to take the place over no problem. They ain't expecting an attack from us, and none of those useless fucks in Home can fight. We'll take them down quickly and the place will be ours."

The others laughed, but none of them spoke. They seemed to all agree on the plan. Nothing left to discuss.

As they walked off, blending into the night when they got far enough away, Vicky looked at Serj. "We need to tell the others," she said. "They need to know what's coming for them before we set the diseased loose. If anything goes wrong, they need to be ready. Besides, I hate to admit it, but you're right about the light. It would be suicide to let the diseased out now."

"But if we tell the others, they'll want to come with us in the morning. What about Scoop and Meisha?"

Vicky chewed the inside of her mouth for a second before she said, "I have a plan."

Chapter Thirty-Six

The light in Home's foyer had shown Scoop asleep against the window where she waited for her daughter's return. Vicky hadn't seen peace on the woman's face for a long time, and maybe they should have let her rest, but they needed all the guards behind this.

At a guess, Vicky assumed it to be past ten in the evening, and although it had been warm earlier, the breeze now chewed on the parts of her body not covered with clothes.

Vicky slipped the key into Home's front door and freed it with a *click*. A look at the window and she saw Scoop's eyes flash open.

When she slipped into the bleach-scented foyer with Serj behind her, Vicky closed the door and looked at her friend.

A screwed-up face and confused frown and Scoop said, "I thought you were Meisha."

The words stabbed into Vicky's chest and she said, "Sorry."

Scoop didn't reply.

"We went out to check on everything and got more than we bargained for."

Still groggy from sleep, her voice croaking as she spoke, Scoop said, "What do you mean?"

"We need to get the guards together in the monitor room to discuss it."

"I ain't going *anywhere*."

"You can look at the monitors for Meisha."

"The monitors are dark."

Vicky made a point to look out of the large window in front of her and then back at Scoop. "Your view will be as good there as it is here. If you see anything, you can leave straight away."

Not that Scoop looked pleased with the plan, but she accepted it with a nod.

Chapter Thirty-Seven

The same size as all of the rooms in Home. The same white walls, the same blue linoleum flooring, the same plain ceiling. Be it a bedroom, a gym, a prison cell, or a surveillance room, each one had to fit into the same cramped space of every room in Home. Other than the communal areas, the rooms were all an identical size. A single bedroom at best, a double at an absolute squeeze.

A wall of monitors, a seat in front of them, and all five of Home's guards meant every time Vicky moved, she bumped into something or someone. Serj, Flynn, and Piotr watched Vicky, waiting for her to speak. Scoop watched the monitors. Although what she could see in the dark …

With her back to the monitors, Vicky faced the others, the screen glow lighting up their features and casting strong shadows in the poorly lit room.

"Serj and I went out about half an hour ago and we saw some people from Moira's community."

"You went out without us *again*?" Flynn said. "Why do you keep on doing that?"

"We wanted to check on everything outside and to walk the route we'll lead the diseased on when we set them loose."

"In the *dark*?"

"It *wasn't* dark when we went out," Vicky said. "Besides, we don't have much time left before they attack us."

Although Flynn drew a breath to reply, and the tension in the room wound tighter from the silent anticipation of it, he kept it to himself.

Serj spoke next, reciting the lie he and Vicky had agreed upon. "They said they're planning to attack us in two days' time." If they told the group they had two days, it would get them ready for an attack should they need to be, but allow Vicky and Serj to take care of things in their own way, without Scoop finding Meisha. If they thought they'd get attacked tomorrow, the guards would be up at the crack of dawn with them.

"They want Home for their own," Serj continued. "I'm guessing that's the only reason the solar panels and our water filtration system have remained intact. Why would they destroy something they plan on using themselves?"

"We need to release the diseased on them before they can do that," Vicky said. The other guards nodded.

Scoop had watched the monitors for the entire time, so when she spoke, Vicky jumped. "When shall we attack them?"

Heat spread through Vicky's cheeks as she lied to them. "Tomorrow. At nine in the morning." If they thought they had a whole day to attack Moira's community, the guards would accept a nine a.m. start.

"How will we all get up at nine?" Flynn asked.

"I've slept all day, so I'll be awake," Vicky said. "I'll get Serj at four for his shift in here, Scoop is taking over from him at six, and Piotr after her at eight. If we need to wake people up, then we can, but we'll be awake in time." Before anyone could speak, Vicky added, "I don't think we should tell the community about it yet. If we can take down Moira and her lot with the penned-in diseased, then we won't need to involve them. Besides, I don't want to tell them about the pen."

Silence met Vicky's comment.

Scoop finally said, "But what if we can't?"

"They'll be ready," Serj said. "Most of the people in Home are preparing for what's coming, so I have no doubt they'll mobilise should they need to. What's important is that we make sure *we're* ready to mobilise them. We're keeping it between the guards for now to save an early panic."

"And will you actually let me do something tomorrow, Vicky?" Flynn said, his shoulders pulled back, his stare fixed on her.

Vicky ignored the comment.

"I hope you're right about this," Scoop then said, her eyes deep and dark pits in her tired face. The thick white bands of her eyeballs stood out beneath her mahogany irises. "Whatever happens, I won't let that community take anything else from me. This world has already taken enough."

Silence followed her comment until she spoke again. "We lost Meisha's dad right at the beginning of all of this. He died so we could survive. He faced the diseased to give us a chance to get away. Now Meisha's gone."

Although Vicky could feel Serj next to her, she didn't look at him. Instead, she looked at the floor. If Scoop stared into her eyes, she'd surely see deceit.

At the sound of Scoop's sobs, Vicky looked up again.

Scoop's shoulders bobbed with her crying and she shook her head. "I pray she's okay. Every waking moment I pray for Meisha."

No one else moved, so Vicky stepped forward and hugged her friend. If it didn't jeopardise everything, she would have told her about her daughter, but they needed to make the decision for the greater good.

While Vicky held Scoop, she looked up at Serj, and Serj stared straight back at her. They didn't communicate with one another, but they didn't need to. They'd agreed they couldn't tell her; they didn't need to discuss it beyond that.

Piotr's thick Russian accent cut through the room, taking some of the focus away from Scoop's distress.

"I had a wife and child too. We hid out in a school for the longest time and we thought we were safe. But one of the community got chased and he broke our number one rule: don't bring any diseased to our door. He broke it and then some. We managed to get him in, but we couldn't keep out the horde he brought with him. There must have been a hundred of them at least. I'd been put on guard duty that night. I was at the opposite end of the school to my wife and son. The diseased rushed in and swarmed the place. I *fought*." The large man shook as he continued, "I *fought* long and hard, but I couldn't do anything to overcome the monsters. There were so many of them, and they got between me and my family."

Tears glistened in Piotr's eyes. "I ran around the outside of the school to get to my wife and son. I knew they would have locked themselves in our room and thought that maybe I could get in through the window. By the time I'd reached the room, I watched the diseased smash the door down and swarm the place. I saw them attack my family." Several tears ran down Piotr's cheeks when he looked at Flynn. "Alexander, or Sasha as we called him, would be your age now."

It suddenly made sense to Vicky to see this side of Piotr. His shut-off nature and coldness except for when he looked after Flynn. "You did everything you could have done," she said.

The large man pulled his shoulders back and lifted his wide chest with a steadying breath as he stared at the bank of monitors. "It doesn't feel like it," he replied.

Silence for what felt like the longest time before Vicky said, "So, we meet in the foyer at nine tomorrow morning." She didn't give the others an opportunity to reply. Instead, she turned around and left the room.

Chapter Thirty-Eight

A disrupted sleeping pattern had left Vicky all over the place. Her eyes stung as if they'd been bathed in chlorine, and she fought to push her panic down every few seconds as it rose inside of her. To sit down made it worse, so she got to her feet and paced up and down in the canteen.

Vicky currently had the space to herself, but that would soon change. Even after years of not having to get up for work, it seemed like at least at third of the community were early risers. As an insomniac, she obsessed about other people's sleeping patterns and always saw the same faces at similar times of day.

A look at the screens on the wall and the time read 5:45. Another five minutes would be ideal, but she couldn't wait any longer.

As Vicky walked down the corridor towards the monitor room, she increased her pace to try to wake herself up and spend some of her nervous energy.

The sharp bite of bleach in the air seemed to make her eyes sting worse than before.

When Vicky got to the monitor room, she looked up and

down the corridor. It seemed clear. She knocked.

It sounded like Serj had been sleeping from the way he said, "Uh … hello?"

Vicky walked in to find him blinking as if trying to wake up, and she raised an eyebrow at him. He blushed but didn't say anything.

"It's ten to six," Vicky said. "I reckon we can go and wake Scoop up now and get her down here."

When Serj stood up, his wheeled chair scooted out away from him. He stretched up to the ceiling and groaned before he bent over and touched his toes.

"We ain't got time for yoga, you know?"

"Nice," Serj said.

"What?"

"I get it, because I'm Indian, I do yoga."

Even with the stress of what lay before them, Vicky smiled. "Do you?"

A sharp sniff and Serj straightened his back. "That's not the point. Don't be so racist!"

When Vicky said nothing in response, Serj snapped, "I'll meet you in the canteen in five minutes. I need to piss first."

"Fine, I'm going to get a crossbow and some hammers for the people in Moira's prison. I'll hide my harness and weapons in the canteen so Scoop doesn't see them."

***

The canteen still remained empty by the time Serj entered, and the screens now read 5:55. As the man walked toward her, Vicky pointed for him to wait in the corner with her things. It would be better if Scoop thought him to still be in the monitor room. She then walked up the short flight of stairs to Home's foyer.

As Vicky had expected, Scoop had fallen asleep again. She walked over to the woman and gently tugged on her shoulder.

Scoop woke up with a deep inhale, her eyes spreading wide and fixing on Vicky. "Have you found her?"

The tiredness returned to Scoop's face when Vicky shook her head and she screwed up her features. "Then why the fuck are you waking me up?"

"It's your turn in the monitor room."

A scowl remained on Scoop's face and Vicky readied herself to defend the woman's attack. But she seemed to wake up a little and shook her head before she got unsteadily to her feet. "I'll go to the toilet and then relieve him."

Vicky smiled in acknowledgement to her.

A second after Scoop left, Serj appeared in the foyer and handed Vicky her things. She slipped her harness on and strapped her crossbow to it, held onto the three small hammers, and unlocked the front door. "I reckon we have five minutes to get out of sight," she said. "She's going to the toilet first, so that gives us a little bit longer to get out of the monitor's field of vision. You ready for this?"

Instead of nodding, Serj raised his eyebrows.

Vicky couldn't argue with him. How could he be ready with what they had to face? "Okay," she said and pulled the door wide, the fresh morning air rushing into the place. "Let's do this."

Chapter Thirty-Nine

The early morning chill lit up Vicky's skin with gooseflesh. Although she'd be bound to warm up soon with the pace her and Serj moved at. The dewy grass soaked her combat trousers and whipped at her thighs as she sprinted through it. Her feet coped with the uneven ground just fine, and she screwed her face up against the light pinpricks from the cold mist.

Vicky pushed on with a new crossbow and harness strapped to her, her knife down the back of her trousers, and three small hammers in her right grip. Once they'd checked on the diseased, she'd drop the hammers with the prisoners in Moira's community. She listened to Serj pant as he ran next to her.

Before long the June sun would burn away the mist, but at six in the morning it would be a little while still. Vulnerable to an attack due to their lack of visibility, neither of them spoke as they looked for the diseased, their breaths turning to condensation in the sharp air.

"Hey!" The sound cut through the still morning. A startled crow cawed as it burst to life beside Vicky.

Vicky spun around, all three hammers raised as she faced the direction of the sound. Not that she needed to panic. Ten years of living with the same person made them easy to identify, whether they were hidden by the mist or not.

Before he appeared, Vicky lowered her hammers.

At first a silhouette, Flynn became more recognisable the closer he walked to them. He threw his arms in the air. "What the *hell* are you two doing? I thought we said nine o'clock."

Although Serj drew a breath to speak, Vicky cut him off. "We're checking on the diseased. We need to make sure everything's okay before we go to Moira's community. And we want to take these to her prisoners." She held up the three hammers.

"Bullshit."

Vicky frowned at him. "Huh?"

"That's bullshit."

"Watch your tongue. And why would I lie about taking the hammers to the prisoners? They need to smash the concrete up so they can get the fence free from it and escape. We need to get these to them before we set the diseased loose."

No more than a metre separated them at that point and Flynn shook his head. "I didn't say you weren't going to drop the hammers off first, but why do it now? Why so early?"

"So I can do it while most of Moira's community sleeps. Do you fancy sneaking down there in broad daylight?"

A shake of his head and Flynn screwed his face up at her. "I've known you ten years, Vicky."

They were now out of the camera's field of vision, so Vicky remained stationary and scanned around for diseased. "What's knowing me for ten years got to do with anything?"

"I know when you're lying. You may have planned on dropping the hammers off with the community, but there's more to it than that. You're planning on letting the diseased out before nine o'clock, aren't you?"

There seemed little point in hiding the truth from him now. "Look, there are a few very good reasons for that."

"Like?"

"Meisha's over there."

Flynn's jaw dropped so quickly it looked like it had instantly dislocated. Once he'd recovered, he said, "Why haven't you told Scoop?"

A look around again and Vicky saw nothing. The sound of the diseased rode on the wind toward them from the pen, but nothing else. "Does she know you've come out here?"

Flynn shook his head. "I don't think so."

Serj stepped forward. "Hopefully he got out before she made it to the monitor room. Does *anyone* know you've come out?"

Another shake of his head.

"Okay," Vicky said. "We've not told Scoop because it won't achieve anything. Meisha's been bitten. If Scoop knew about that, she'd want to get her out and we can't afford to do that."

"She's in the pen?"

Vicky looked at Serj, who seemed to be dividing his time between the argument in front of him and their surroundings. "Yes, but it's not her daughter anymore. What's trapped in that pen is a twisted version of the beautiful girl we all knew. She's no more than a poisoned shell now. A rotting mess that doesn't even know she's Meisha."

Flynn paused and stared at Vicky. "And what was the other good reason for you lying?"

Vicky said, "You."

"*Me?*"

Tension gripped Vicky's shoulders and lifted them to her neck. "Look, you're not going to like this."

"Just spit it out."

"I wanted to protect you."

A shake of his head and Flynn pulled his hair from his eyes. The sides of his jaw tensed and relaxed as he glared at her. "When will you let me grow up?"

The genesis of tears itched Vicky's eyes. Her vision blurred. "I'm not sure I ever can. Whenever I want to let you take more responsibility, I think of your mum and dad. I think about what they would do and how they would feel if my decision led to your death."

"You can't protect me forever, Vicky."

"No, but that doesn't mean I don't want to try."

"I'm coming with you," Flynn said and he walked off towards the pen.

Vicky caught up with him. "No, you're *not*. You need to go back to Home."

"If you don't let me come with you, I'll go back to the community, and I'll tell them everything."

Vicky looked at Flynn and then at Serj, who had also fallen into stride with them. What could she do? A deep sigh and she shook her head at him. "You listen to what we say, okay?"

Flynn nodded.

"I'm being serious. I don't want any of your jumped-up teenager bullshit."

Flynn nodded again.

"Right."

The sound of the diseased had already grown louder for the few metres they moved forward. Maybe they'd been resting before. Maybe they'd heard the argument and had grown agitated. Whatever the reason, they seemed riled.

"I'm still not happy about this," Vicky said as they crested the hill just before the pen. "And you're not coming to Moira's community with me. You and Serj can wait here while I …" She didn't finish her sentence.

Although Vicky focused in front of her, she didn't need to look at Serj and Flynn to know they'd be doing the same. Despite opening and closing her mouth, she couldn't find the words.

Serj did a pretty good job when he said, "Fuck! They've got out."

"Or they've been *let* out," Flynn said.

Chapter Forty

Vicky stood frozen to the spot as she stared straight ahead. The other two on either side of her did the same. They all watched the diseased wander through the mist. Limp jawed, limp limbed, and uncoordinated, the monsters moved with an aimless ramble, ready to focus their hive mind on whatever presented itself to them.

"Who do you think did it?" Flynn said, leaning close to Vicky so she could hear his whisper.

"Who do you *think*?" Vicky replied.

Serj shook his head. "We should have let them out sooner. You know what, fuck it. After all the effort we've put in, maybe we should still lead them to Moira's community."

The clouds of condensation formed in front of Vicky with more frequency than before as her breathing sped up. Driven by her rapid pulse, she tried to slow it down, but she had no control over her panic at that moment. She lifted the hammers. "How will I get these to the prisoners?"

"It might be too late for them," Serj said.

"But I made a promise." Vicky shook her head and spoke to

the ground. "I should have freed them days ago."

"We need to do something. Standing here like lemons won't help us." When Flynn spoke, he'd raised his voice a little bit too loud and it carried across the quiet morning.

Vicky's heart beat in her neck to see one of the diseased spin around and stare straight at him. Recognition—or as close to recognition as could register on the diseased's face with its eyes still dead and jaw still limp—lit it up and it opened its mouth.

"Come on," Vicky hissed as she tugged on Flynn's shoulder.

By the time the diseased loosed its scream, the three of them had spun on their heels and were sprinting back towards Home's entrance.

Just a few steps into their retreat, one scream turned into many.

Vicky had been here before countless times, but not often with Flynn beside her. She'd heard someone say they didn't know fear until they had children. She finally understood that.

The long grass dragged on Vicky's retreat. The diseased had to run the same path as them. Surely it would slow them down too. Enraged screams came after them in a wave.

A glance behind and Vicky nearly lost the strength in her legs. The pack had seemed numerous when penned, but now it looked like twice the amount.

Vicky turned back around and faced the entryway to Home, every footstep rolling as it coped with the undulations in the ground.

When Vicky got a few steps closer, she saw the mist had cleared a little, revealing the sign above the entryway to Home. The others clearly saw it too because Flynn uttered a breathless, "What the hell?"

A huge white banner—a sheet or something similar—painted red. From the distance between them and the banner, it looked like blood. If Vicky knew Moira at all, they'd probably find out whose fairly soon. It read *We've found your pets. Now it's time for you to join them.*

Another look behind. Maybe they'd gained on them, Vicky couldn't tell, but she couldn't let up either.

The sound of her own ragged breaths rang through Vicky's head as she sprinted, and she pulled her door key from around her neck. A stampede behind them, she couldn't quite feel the thud of their feet through the ground, but much closer and it would shake as if an earthquake ran through it. The reek of rot had caught up to her, and with every lungful she inhaled the noxious stench. It damn near gagged her.

Before Vicky could pull the key from around her neck—her damp trousers chafing on her thighs as she ran—the door to Home opened and Scoop stood in the doorway. It gave Vicky the extra burst she needed and she opened up a gap between her and the other two, running into Home before them.

Once in the foyer, Vicky spun around and called out, "Come on! Hurry up. They're gaining on you."

Flynn looked almost as pained as the mob of diseased chasing him. He winced, his mouth open wide from the effort of the sprint.

Everything seemed to drop into slow motion at that point. Like Vicky had done, Flynn turned around to look at the mob behind him as he ran. Although, unlike Vicky, he tripped as he looked over his shoulder. One moment, Vicky watched him run, the next he vanished into the long grass.

Serj—who ran next to Flynn—continued on, clearly oblivious to his fall. He sprinted into Home like Vicky had.

"Where's Flynn?" Serj said once he'd spun around, his entire body rising and falling with his gasps.

Vicky didn't answer him. Instead, she darted outside and sprinted towards the fallen Flynn. Hammers still in hand, she wound them back and swung them into the jaw of the diseased at the front of the pack. Two more came at her and Vicky dealt with them, each blow from the heavy metal tools cracking as they sank into a jaw and then a cheekbone. Blood sprayed away from the impact both times and the second and third diseased fell to the ground.

Before any more could jump them, Vicky reached down to Flynn, took his hand and pulled him to his feet.

The boy seemed hurt and unable to put pressure on his ankle. Hopefully no more than a twist, Vicky shoved him back toward Home. "Go, now. I'll cover you."

Vicky faced the diseased again and swung for the monsters as they descended on her. Each blow scored a hit and each blow drained her energy that little bit more than the previous one. No way could she fight them all.

Vicky took down the seventh and eighth diseased, the vibration down the handle of the hammers making her hands buzz. Now she'd taken down the lead runners, she didn't have long before the rest of the pack caught up.

When Vicky looked behind to see Flynn had stumbled into Home, she took off after him.

The second Vicky sprinted through Home's front door, Serj slammed it shut and slid the bolts across.

The only sound for the next few seconds came from the heavy breaths of the three as they recovered from their run. A few moments later the loud *booms* of the diseased crashed into Home's front door and windows. One after the other, they peppered the front of Home like a meteor shower.

Scoop spoke first. She pressed her face against one of Home's large windows and tilted her head to the side as her voice cracked. "*Meisha?*"

Chapter Forty-One

"I'm not letting you out," Vicky said as she stood in front of Home's exit. Serj and Flynn flanked her, the three of them united against Scoop's fury.

"My fucking *daughter's* out there!"

"She's not your daughter anymore," Vicky said. "What do you hope to achieve by going out there?"

Scoop continued to pace as she had done for the past fifteen minutes, staring out of the window as she moved back and forth. Many of the diseased had moved away from the front door, but Meisha remained close, almost as if she knew she had once belonged inside.

After a glance at the other two, Vicky moved over to Scoop and they both stopped to stare out of the window. "Look at her."

"You think I'm not?"

"That's *not* Meisha."

"What would you do if that was Flynn out there?"

When Vicky didn't answer, Scoop turned to her, clenched her fists, pulled her shoulders back, and jutted her chin out. Her voice came out as a low growl that turned the air between them electric. "Let me out."

"If we let you out"—Vicky pointed at the window—"we're letting *them* in."

"I'll get out quickly," Scoop said. "They've backed away from the door now. Open it a crack and I'll run out and get them to chase me. Then you can close the door and lock it behind me."

"It won't work."

"*Make* it work! Because if you don't let me out now, I'll get out sooner or later, and I'll make sure I leave that fucking door open behind me."

Two gentle snaps called through the foyer as Serj undid the bolts at the top and bottom of the door. For a moment he and Vicky stared at each other before he turned to Scoop. "You need to be ready to run."

"What are you *doing*?" Vicky said.

"Letting Scoop do what she wants to do. She's an adult, Vick."

"But she's too distraught to think straight. She can't do this. It's suicide."

"She's an adult."

"What about everyone in Home? What if we let them in?"

"They're far enough away. Besides, they'll chase *her*, I'm sure."

A final glance at Scoop and Scoop nodded. "Just let me do this," she said. "I need to get to my little girl."

"She's not your little girl anymore."

"She *is*."

The clenched jaw, the creased brow, and the dark stare told Vicky everything she needed to know. Scoop would do this regardless of what she said. Nothing would change her mind. Nothing.

Vicky shook her head, walked over to Scoop and pulled her into a tight hug. "Be ready to get out as quickly as you can."

Scoop squeezed Vicky back and Vicky felt her nodding into her neck.

After she'd handed the hammers to Flynn, Vicky pulled her crossbow from her back and pressed the stock into her shoulder. She looked down her weapon at the front door and said, "You ready?"

Scoop and Serj both nodded.

Vicky tried to push her grief to one side with a heavy sigh and said, "Take care of yourself, Scoop." Tears swelled inside of her. To say goodbye would set them loose and she still needed to see. Maybe they should have told her sooner, but maybe Scoop would have sacrificed herself sooner had she known. Too many good people had gone from this world already.

Vicky could do nothing to stop her flow of tears as Serj gripped the front door's handle. "Three," he said.

The tension wound tight in the foyer and Vicky pulled a dry gulp into her arid throat.

"Two …"

Vicky's finger shook on the trigger of her crossbow.

"One."

Serj pulled the door open about thirty centimetres wide. The closest diseased stood about two metres away. Vicky unloaded a bolt into its face. It scored a direct hit and drove the rancid fucker back a step.

As the beast screamed, Scoop ran out, body-checked it, and took the attention of the rest with her.

Serj slammed the door behind her and bolted the locks again. He exhaled hard enough to blow his cheeks out and shared a look with Vicky.

Vicky moved to the window, her face damp with tears, to watch her friend push through the dense pack of bodies as the ravenous mob climbed over one another to get at her.

Scoop swung for them, shoved them, and kicked out. Maybe she'd already been bitten by the time she got to her daughter, but when she arrived at Meisha, she still had all the traits of the living. At that moment, she gave up defending herself and wrapped her arms around the girl.

If Vicky could judge anything by the look on Meisha's face, it would be that she didn't recognise her mother. Maybe her inclination to remain close to Home had been a coincidence. Like all of the other diseased, she seemed lost in the torment of the plague. She pulled into her mother's hug, spread her mouth wide, and bit into her neck.

Scoop didn't show the pain she undoubtably felt. Instead, she clung to her daughter as blood spread from the bite mark out over her clothes, turning her khaki guard shirt dark.

When Meisha took a second bite into Scoop's neck, Vicky turned away and looked at both Serj and Flynn. They too cried freely, their eyes bloodshot, their cheeks glistening with their tears. They should have told Scoop sooner.

Chapter Forty-Two

The four remaining guards stood together in Home's foyer. Serj, Flynn, Piotr, and Vicky. Vicky looked at the other three and then the space where Scoop should have been. It somehow filled the rest of the area. A quiet, yet vigilant observer, she'd offered a calm reassurance that she had anyone's back should they need it.

Serj walked along the line of guards and gave each of them a silver key. "The new lock has been fitted." When he got to the nail on the wall, he hung up two keys where there had previously only been one.

A heavy sigh to Vicky's right and she looked at Flynn. He bit his bottom lip and his eyes glazed. Vicky reached across to hug him and he stepped a pace away from her, throwing her a dark scowl. The rejection sank through her heart, but she lifted her chin and stepped back. Even after what they'd just been through, she still couldn't be the one to offer him comfort.

"We need to go and talk to them, then," Serj said as he nodded in the direction of the canteen. "They need answers."

"And you have some, do you?" Piotr's deep voice echoed in the foyer.

Serj shrugged. "Come on," he said. "I'll think of something."

***

The back wall felt cold to the touch as Vicky leaned against it with Piotr next to her and Flynn next to him. Were it a Tuesday morning, then she'd be addressing the people of Home. They had a weekend to get through before it got to Tuesday again. Maybe she'd already led her final training session.

As what seemed to be the last of the people of Home filled the canteen, Serj stood still and stared at the wall of monitors. No matter which angle they flicked to, scores of diseased milled about outside the complex. The people of Home looked at the monitors too.

"I'm sure I don't need to tell you we have a problem outside," Serj said. "We don't know where the diseased came from, but my guess would be that Moira had something to do with it."

Vicky's cheeks heated up at the lie and she felt Flynn stare across at her. No doubt she glowed red for everyone to see, but she couldn't hide it. A look across at Piotr and then Flynn and she met the same dark judgment from both of them, although Piotr hid it slightly better.

The silence threatened to crawl up from the ground and throttle Vicky, but Serj broke it before she had to tap out.

"If you don't know by now, Scoop didn't make it."

Tears itched Vicky's eyes and she watched the monitors to see if her friend appeared on them. The people of Home didn't need to see that. None of them did.

"Meisha went out on her own the other day," Serj said, "and when the diseased attacked, Meisha got caught up in it. Scoop saw her infected daughter and ran to her. She knew Meisha was gone, and the monster that remained wasn't her, but she couldn't control her impulses. She died within three steps of Home's front door."

Vicky felt sick with grief as she looked from the monitors to Serj to the judgment of Piotr and Flynn. The intensity of Flynn's glare and how he leaned toward her made it look like he wanted to say something, but he'd managed to keep it to himself. So far anyway. One word from him and everything would come crashing down. The boy had a hot head. Hopefully he could keep himself in check.

All the while Serj spoke to the crowd, he paced up and down the crash mats. Even with the gravity of their situation, Vicky wanted to tell him to take his shoes off, but she refrained. They probably wouldn't need to train again anyway.

One of the men from Home stepped forward. Brian maybe? Vicky couldn't remember his name. There were so many people at Home she'd barely spoken to. A tall man, at least six feet and three inches, he had long thick hair and a bushy beard. "How are we supposed to fight them *and* Moira?"

The silence hung in the vast space and Serj continued to pace up and down. He looked like he had an answer for them, and then he said, "I dunno. Honestly, I don't have a clue."

Some of the people looked at one another, and when Vicky scanned the crowd, she saw Sally; the woman she'd rescued from Hugh's eviction. The same worried frown dominated her features as it did everyone else's.

"However—" Serj stopped and raised a finger in the air "—what I do know is that if we don't find a way to do it, we'll die and Moira will take this place for her own."

The statement threw a sombre blanket over the room and everyone sank beneath its weight. They weren't ready to go to war. They would never be ready to go to war. Of all the people Vicky had trained, only a handful of them had learned how to fight. The rest would have to pick it up pretty damn quick. If they even had it in them. Maybe they'd be presenting themselves for the slaughter.

The man Vicky thought of as Brian, regardless of his name, spoke up again. "But if we leave them alone, then they may leave *us* alone." He looked across at the monitors and the diseased displayed on them. "We've existed side by side with Moira's community for *years* now." When he stared at Vicky, she felt a chill snap through her. "We've only had a problem with them since *she's* been here."

The static crowd came to life. Nods and noises of agreement filled the air.

Sharon Blythe stepped forward. "I agree," she said. "My children are dead because of her."

Dan Blythe moved next to his wife and stared hatred at Vicky. "I think she's a fucking liability."

The quiet murmur of concurrence grew in volume and a few people said *Yeah* or *I agree* or *We were fine without her*.

When Brian pointed at Vicky again, his thick hair and beard wobbled with his fury. "*She's* brought this down on us. If it wasn't for her, we'd be doing fine now."

The heat in Vicky's cheeks rushed straight to her gut and she pushed off from the wall. She slammed a clenched right fist against her open left palm. "No, you wouldn't! And you know why? Because sooner or later, Moira will take this community for her own. You had Hugh kicking innocent people out and Moira standing by waiting for the right time to take over. I didn't bring that here, that existed long before me. If Moira had wanted to simply attack Home, the solar panels would have been destroyed by now. But she wants more than that and always has. Like Serj said, she wants Home for her own. Me being here hasn't changed that. What's your name?" she said to Brian.

"Brian," he responded. She should have given herself more credit for remembering it.

"Well, you know what, Brian? If she takes this place over, you'll wish you'd fought now. I've seen what she does to prisoners, so believe me when I say you don't want to be one of them. I can leave now if you all want me to, but whether I came here or not, this community was fucked."

A few people gasped at Vicky's statement. "The only difference between then and now is then you were fucking ignorant." She walked closer to Brian so only a metre of blue crash mat separated them. "Now you know what's coming for you."

Before Brian could react, Flynn stepped forward. "I agree, and I'm with you, Vicky."

Vicky looked at Flynn, who returned her glare with the same anger he'd looked at her with for weeks now. He certainly didn't forgive her, but he wouldn't sell her out either.

Brian sneered at Flynn and it took all of Vicky's patience to refrain from knocking the sneer from his face. He shook his head and said, "Of course *you* agree—"

"Me too," Piotr said, cutting the hairy man off mid-sentence.

Brian drew a deep breath and opened his mouth to reply, but Serj cut him short this time. "And me."

Until that point only the guards had stepped forward. When Stuart stepped from the group of people in Home, Brian's shoulders slumped. "And me," he said.

Sally stepped forward. "And me."

The wind had been well and truly robbed from Brian's sails. Even if he had the majority on his side at that moment, only Sharon and Dan seemed willing to voice it. The tension in the room wound a notch tighter, but before anyone else could speak, a loud scream cut through Home. It rushed down the corridors and into the canteen. It sounded like a man in agony.

Chapter Forty-Three

The crowd parted for Vicky as she rushed through them in the direction of the sound. The man screamed again, his shrill call bouncing off the walls of the complex.

Even as she passed the screens, Vicky got a sense of the sheer weight of diseased outside without directly looking at them.

As Vicky ran, she heard footsteps follow her. A glance over her shoulder and she saw Piotr, Serj, and even Flynn, who moved more freely than he'd done since his fall.

Vicky swerved through several of the dining tables before she jumped up on a bench of one and onto the Formica top. She watched for plates and glasses, but managed to hop from table to table without slipping. Although she didn't turn around, the sound of the guards' thumping steps followed behind her.

The slap of her feet rang out when she jumped from the last table and landed on the hard floor. She darted for the corridor where the sound came from.

Vicky stopped dead the second she looked down the hallway.

A moment later, Piotr crashed into the back of her and

shoved Vicky forward a step closer to them. The other two guards caught up.

"What the—?" Flynn said through his heavy breaths.

The white walls of the corridor had been painted red and glistened with the spilled blood of what must have been the man. Where he'd screamed before, he now stood silent, pinned to the wall by a woman feasting on his throat. She seemed oblivious to her spectators.

When Vicky saw a little boy huddled away from the pair, she pulled her knife from the back of her trousers and stepped forward. Fuck knew if he'd been bitten or not. He didn't move, whatever that meant.

Even though Vicky tried to be quiet, the pads of her feet touched the blue linoleum floor as she walked. If she could get the child and pull him away, it didn't matter what noise she made afterwards. She'd have to fight the diseased anyway, but better she saved the child if she could.

The guards behind Vicky must have remained still because she could only hear the sound of the woman as she feasted on the man. A gristly snapping and squelching sound as if she was chewing through wet bone.

It didn't matter how close Vicky got to the boy, she couldn't work him out. Soaked in the blood coating the walls, he continued to huddle in a ball and not look up.

Vicky got to within a few metres of the boy when the sound of footsteps rushed across the end of the corridor. She didn't look back. The people from the canteen must have run over to watch. No doubt none of them would help.

When one of the people gasped, the woman and the boy

both looked up. They both stared at Vicky with the same bleeding eyes of the diseased. "Fuck," she said and lunged for the boy as he lunged for her.

It might have only been a six-inch blade, but when Vicky drove it into the boy's right eye, it sank deep enough to turn him limp.

The slap of the woman's footsteps came at Vicky as she shoved the boy aside.

The woman waved her arms in Vicky's direction, blood dripping from her chin and the thick reek of rot coming forward with her.

In the tight space Vicky only had one chance.

The woman yelled and dived at Vicky.

Vicky dropped to the ground, kicked the vile creature in the stomach as she passed over her, and listened to her land on the other side of her with an *oomph*.

Before the creature could recover, Vicky sprang to her feet, rushed her, and finished her off in the same way she'd just dispatched the child.

As much as she wanted to stop there, Vicky headed over to the man, breathing hard as she moved. He sat slumped against the wall, motionless as if he'd passed out.

When Vicky got to him, he opened his bloody eyes.

The crack of his skull popped through the space when Vicky plunged her knife into the top of his head. His mouth fell loose and his eyes dribbled fresh blood.

The corpse fell from his sitting position when Vicky stepped away from him, and slapped down against the linoleum as a discarded carcass.

The chatter at the other end of the corridor sounded like quite a few people had gathered to watch. Instead of turning to face them, Vicky walked away from the carnage and in the direction of her room.

Serj's voice filled the hallway. "You still think Vicky's the problem? I'd say she's pretty damn useful to us when you look at what she just did. What no one else was prepared to do. Also, how the *hell* did someone get in here with the disease? Anyone coming back to Home now will be searched for bite marks before they enter the place. If you get bitten, it's game over. Don't be so fucking selfish as to come back. You're *not* the exception; you *will* fucking turn."

In all the time she'd been in Home, Vicky hadn't witnessed Serj lose it often. She didn't look back, but she couldn't hear anything from the people he addressed.

"You, you, and you," Serj said. "Clean up this mess.

Vicky stepped into her room and closed the door behind herself. It didn't silence the sound of the people outside, but it shut them off enough. More importantly, it showed them she didn't want to talk.

Chapter Forty-Four

When Vicky grabbed the door handle to leave her room, it felt cold to the touch and gooseflesh ran up her right arm. The corridor had been a mess the last time she'd been in it. Although a few hours had passed since then. A deep breath and she pulled the door wide as she exhaled. The hinges creaked, calling out into the hallway.

The white corridor shone as white as always, but the bleach smelled so strong Vicky ruffled her nose in response to it. There remained no trace of the blood she'd seen only a few hours previously, the blood she'd helped paint the walls with.

Voices mixed together as a hum of chatter and came down the corridor from the canteen area. What would the people say to her when they saw her? Would she be a hero for doing the job no one else wanted, or a monster for her actions? In the other direction Vicky heard the crash and bang of pans. The kitchen staff never spoke to her, not even when she tried to engage them in conversation, so she headed in that direction.

The second Vicky stepped into the vast area, the sounds stopped and the chefs looked up at her. "Well, this has never happened before," she said from the side of her mouth as she froze under the collective gaze of the staff.

When none of them replied, Vicky looked at the floor. She walked toward the other corridor that ran parallel to the one she'd just stepped out of. It had the monitor room along it.

In the next corridor, a woman Vicky recognised but didn't know the name of walked towards her. As Vicky had just done in the kitchen, the woman looked down. She also pressed herself against the wall at Vicky's passing.

It made it easier than having to talk to her. Before Vicky could bump into anyone else, she came to the monitor room's door, pulled it open, and entered.

To see Flynn in the room sent Vicky's heart and stomach south. Instead of looking at the boy, she looked at the wall of monitors and shook her head. Diseased on every screen. *Multiple* diseased on every screen. They shuffled around, snapping at the air as a dog would when catching a fly. Fuck knew how they'd get through them should they need to.

A look at Flynn and she saw he focused on the monitors too. "We need to go outside and deal with this at some point."

"Good luck persuading the people to do that."

"Do you have any other suggestions?" Vicky asked.

"No, but we wouldn't have needed them had you and Serj not filled a pen full of those monsters."

As much as Vicky wanted to shout at the boy, she stared at him and clenched her jaw. She bit so hard it ran pains to her temples.

"I only stood by you in the canteen because I didn't want everyone to turn on you," Flynn said. "Even if you *did* deserve it."

"*You* should try running this place."

"Serj runs it, not you."

"Yeah, right!"

As he threw his shoulders up in a shrug, Flynn said, "Whatever. Just know I'm still pissed about many things, including the monsters outside." He turned to the monitors and looked from one to the next. "You and Serj are responsible for this. They wouldn't be out there were it not for you two."

Vicky couldn't hold back. "Stop being such a self-righteous prick. You wouldn't be here had I not saved your arse out there when you fell over."

At times like this, Vicky remembered the little boy of ten years ago had grown to the size of a man as he towered over her, a faint whiff of body odour coming from him. "And I bet you *loved* that, didn't you? Any chance to make me feel weak and vulnerable, eh?"

Vicky took a step back from Flynn's imposing frame. Not that he'd do anything to her. "I *saved* you, Flynn. And I'd do it again. It's why I wanted you to team up with Piotr so I didn't have to make those decisions anymore. Your life is more important to me than my own. I will *always* put your safety first. Besides, the diseased only chased us because of the noise *you* made."

"They wouldn't have been there in the first place were it not for you! Okay, you saved me, well done."

"And I'd do it again."

"You're not my mother, you know? How many times do I have to remind you?"

"As many times as you like. It won't make any difference.

Regardless of what you think, Flynn, Serj and I did what we thought was best for the community."

"Well, that didn't work, did it? Maybe you two morons shouldn't be in charge if you thought that was best."

The word *moron* hit a nerve and Vicky locked tight. She turned away from Flynn. "Just go back to your room. Get some rest, yeah? God knows you need it. You've always been cranky when you get tired."

"Fuck you, Vicky."

Before Vicky could reply, Flynn stormed out of the room, slamming the door behind him as he left.

Chapter Forty-Five

A couple hours after Flynn left the control room, Vicky continued to watch the monitors. The black and white grainy images became harder to see as night settled in. Although they still had a good few hours before it got dark. Maybe tiredness played a role too. As she stared at the screens—her eyes stinging—more and more diseased appeared with every passing moment. What would they do if they kept coming? At what point would there be so many they couldn't get out the front door?

The meadow in front of Home had diseased everywhere Vicky looked. They trudged through the long grass, aimless in their movement, but still not clearing out. Either side of Home looked the same.

More diseased wandered through the solar panels and Vicky squinted to watch them. They weren't destructive against anything but people, but a shitload of the clumsy fuckers could cause a lot of unintentional damage, and Home relied on that power more than anything.

A look back at the images out the front of Home again and Vicky paused. "What the—?"

To be certain of what she saw, she leaned closer to the monitor in front of her.

Two diseased, locked together almost as if embracing one another. More than likely they were fighting, but as Vicky studied them, her heart beat harder than before and a rock clamped tight in her stomach.

The only sound in the room came from the buzz of electrical devices surrounding her and the pounding of her own pulse. The image might have been poor quality, but that didn't matter. Vicky recognised what she saw from the start and now she had to accept the truth of it. In front of her—locked in one last desperate hug—stood Meisha and Scoop. She gasped. "No way!"

A knock on the door sent Vicky's pulse skyrocketing. Her heart beat like a hamster's as she took deep breaths to try to settle herself down.

After a second knock, she walked over to the door.

When she opened it, the huge figure of Piotr blocked any extra light from coming in. Vicky looked up at him and her heart sank. Of all the people to turn up when she'd just seen *that* outside.

Piotr said nothing as he and Vicky stared at one another. He then looked over her shoulder at the monitors.

The image of the two diseased must have stood out among the rambling chaos because Piotr noticed it immediately. He walked over to it and stared for a few seconds before he said, "Is that …?"

Vicky nodded and cleared the lump in her throat. "Yep."

"Damn."

Another hot wave of sadness rose beneath Vicky's skin, setting fire to her cheeks. "At least they still love each other, I suppose, even after they've turned. Maybe there is still something there. Although I'm not sure Flynn would want much to do with me were we in that state."

Vicky squirmed under Piotr's scrutiny. "The same thing happened between my brother and his kid, you know?"

"Huh?"

"The way Flynn's pushing you away. I saw my nephew do the same to my brother. I think most teenagers do it against their parents."

To be called his parent set Vicky's tears loose and her bottom lip bent out of shape. She wiped them away with the back of her hand and sniffed hard. "I'm sorry," she said as she looked at the floor. "I'm in a bit of a state at the moment."

Piotr waited for Vicky to look up at him. "You do an amazing job with him, you know? You make him feel secure, which allows him to get shitty with you."

An ironic laugh and Vicky shook her head. "That's what it is, is it?"

"Absolutely." After he reached out and lifted her hands in his, his grip firm and warm, Piotr said, "Just keep going, keep loving him, and he'll come round. He'll see it for what it is in time."

The kindness from what had been a cold man up until that point broke Vicky and she could do nothing to stop from crying. This time she didn't try to fight it and let her tears run down her face and off her chin. She shook as she spoke. "I couldn't do anything different even if I tried."

Piotr gripped her in a hug so tight Vicky felt her skeleton shift. She made a gargling noise, more because she felt uncomfortable from the gesture than anything else.

"I know," Piotr said. "And know just how wonderful that is."

Another wave of grief threw Vicky off and she nodded. "Thank you. I needed to hear that."

Before Piotr could reply, Vicky looked away from him. She glanced at the monitor that looked out over the field with the solar panels and her tears stopped instantly. "Oh, shit."

"What?" Piotr said as he followed her line of sight to the monitor.

But she didn't need to tell him.

A gang of about fifteen people, both men and women, had entered the solar panel field from the back. They were carrying weapons from bats to swords to axes. They smashed three panels as Vicky watched on and they looked like they were going for more.

Vicky shook her head. "Looks like I was wrong about them not attacking our electricity supply."

"Fuck!" Piotr said. "What are we going to do?"

"We only have one choice, right?"

After a heavy sigh, Piotr straightened his considerable frame and lifted his chest. He nodded at Vicky. "Come on, then, let's take this fight to them."

Vicky nodded back, drew a deep breath and left the room. Piotr followed behind her.

Chapter Forty-Six

By the time Vicky arrived in the canteen, she'd already loaded up with weapons from the armoury.

Piotr walked by her side, and he too had equipped himself for the fight.

With a crossbow strapped to her back, a baseball bat in her tight grip, and a knife down the back of her trousers, Vicky looked at the people gathered there.

Most of the complex seemed to be in the room at that moment. Well over half of them turned to look at her and Piotr. The rest stood and watched the large monitors on the wall. Not only did they show the diseased waiting outside for them, but they also showed the group of humans smashing up their solar panels whenever they flicked to the view behind Home. Serj and Flynn stood among the crowd.

A dry pinch in her throat, Vicky swallowed and then coughed.

When Serj turned to look at her, Vicky shouted across at him, "We need to get out there and fight."

At first Serj didn't reply, the colour draining from his dark face.

"You've seen what they're doing, right?" Vicky said as she pointed at the screens. "We stay here and do nothing and we'll end up with no power. We *have* to fight them."

Although Serj drew a breath to reply, a dissenting voice came at Vicky across the canteen. "That's easy for you to say." Brian—the tall New Age hippy—stood with Sharon, Dan, and a few others by his side. They should split them up. Too much time together and the paranoid fucks could start a revolution based on ill-informed conspiracy theories. The same hostility that Brian directed at her also came from the people around him. Disdain, revulsion, and open resentment, they looked like they still had a lot of things to say to her.

A furious pulse damn near rocked Vicky where she stood. Tension wound the muscles in her back so tight it hurt, and before she had control of herself, she shouted at them, "Why the *fuck* is it easy for me to say? You think I *want* to go out there in this mess? You think I enjoy this bullshit because I'm one of the only ones brave enough to actually do something about it?"

No less hostile, Brian pulled his shoulders back and Vicky picked up on all the people around the canteen watching them at that moment. "*You* created this mess."

"What the fuck?" Some of Vicky's anger left her. Did they know about the virus and the Alpha Tower?

Before Vicky could say anything, Dan stepped forward. "He has a point. We were fine until you came here."

At least they didn't know the truth. "*Fine?* You had a psycho running this place. He wanted to kick out everyone he deemed to be weak. It would have been easier than fixing the problems in the community like a lack of food from the farm. He simply wanted to reduce numbers. You *miss* that, do you?"

Dan opened his mouth to speak, but Vicky cut him off. "That was a rhetorical question. Not only did you have Hugh fucking shit up, but you also had Moira's community not too far away. You've seen first-hand what she's capable of in what she's done to your children. Now, you may have *felt* you were fine, but you were ignorant to the dangers you lived with, nothing else. How many times do I have to say it?"

Not giving any of them a chance to reply, Vicky said, "Another rhetorical question. You have one fucking choice. Survive or *don't* survive. That's it. If you want power and fresh air down here, we need to fight for those solar panels." She turned to look at the screens and saw the wreck of several more panels as Moira's guards moved forward again.

A look at Brian's narrowed eyes and Vicky said, "Those fuckers are attacking our lifeblood." She looked at Sharon, Dan, and the other sheep that had joined their cause. "I, for one, will not stand around and wait to gas out like fish on a riverbank as our air supply runs out."

Serj and Flynn had already moved toward the corridor with the armoury on it.

"You want revenge for what happened to your children?" Vicky said, this time addressing Sharon.

Sharon nodded.

Vicky pointed a strong finger at the screen again. "Well, there it fucking is." Fuelled by her heavy pulse, she raised her voice. "We need to fuck them up. We need to show them they can't do this to us. Otherwise, they'll roll the fuck over us and take everything we have.

"You can stand here with your mouths open like dumb fish all day—" Vicky looked around the canteen and saw some of the people bristle as if they were energising for the fight "—but I'm going out there to make sure they don't take this place."

An itch burned Vicky's throat as she continued to shout at the people from Home. "Serj and Flynn have just gone to get weapons. You have spears up here, but if there's anything else you need to take, go and see them now."

Stuart, the first of the spectators to move, walked in the same direction Serj and Flynn had just gone in. In that moment Vicky's heart damn near stopped because he looked like the only one who'd go.

A few seconds later another person followed him—a young woman probably still in her twenties. From the look of it, nerves had turned her face pale and sweat beaded on her brow. But she did it, unlike the spineless fucks who seemed more hung up on complaining than anything else.

Within a few minutes, only the complainers remained. A facetious smile, and Vicky said, "It looks like you're outnumbered. Now go and get your fucking weapons, you cowardly fucks."

"And if we say no?" Brian asked.

"You get thrown outside without anything to defend yourself with. It's your choice, but either way, you're not snaking out of the fight we have in front of us. Especially when everyone else is stepping up."

Silence met Vicky's words, but it only lasted for a few seconds before some of the hangers-on to Brian, Sharon, and Dan's group walked in the direction of the armoury.

A few more seconds and Brian shook his head as he walked

past Vicky in the same direction. A low growl as he spoke from the side of his mouth. "You'd best win this fucking fight."

Although Vicky balled her fists, she refrained from knocking the prick out. She could do that when they got back.

Chapter Forty-Seven

Much later and they'd be fighting in the dark. The sun sat low in the sky, but it still lit up the landscape, highlighting just how many diseased loitered outside of Home's main entrance.

After Vicky had watched the monsters through the window for a few more seconds, she looked at the people around her. Most of Home's residents seemed to have gathered there and none of them spoke. From a quick scan, she couldn't tell who hadn't turned up. To Brian, Sharon, and Dan's credit, they all stood in the crowd. Their faces—like most of the others—were pale and locked tight.

Maybe the only people who hadn't come were the old and the young. Vicky preferred to believe that, even if it weren't true.

Vicky looked at the gathered crowd, then Serj, who stood by the front door, and then it came flooding back to her. The attention of the people was focused on her, but she had to ask him. "Serj, is the banner still up?"

Some confused faces looked on, but no one questioned it.

A shake of his head and Serj said, "Flynn and I sorted it out while you were resting."

Vicky exhaled; if the group didn't want to lynch her already, that fucking banner from Moira would have stirred things up.

Before Vicky could say anything else, Serj broke the silence by addressing the crowd. "You ready?"

Many people nodded, but they still didn't speak.

Although he'd asked the group, Serj's eyes settled on Vicky. She nodded too. "Let's do this."

The lock clicked as Serj undid it with his key. He then pulled the two large bolts at the top and bottom of the door free. The rub of metal over metal ended in a *crack* as each one came loose.

Vicky watched through the window to see the diseased respond to the sounds. As stupid as they were, they clearly knew they should pay attention to what was about to step outside.

Anxiety sent butterflies through Vicky's stomach as she continued to watch them. About thirty in total, their rage boiled just beneath the surface, sending them swaying, twitching, and lashing out at thin air. A well-organised fighting unit would take them down without a problem. Sadly, the people of Home weren't a well-organised fighting unit. And they still had the people smashing up the solar panels to contend with.

After a nod at Vicky, Serj yanked the door wide. The sound of the enraged diseased rushed into the place. The noise rode the back of their rotten stench and Vicky saw several of the people from Home step back a pace as if shoved by the wave of funk. None of them were as used to the smell as the four guards were.

Vicky elbowed past the couple of people in front of her and led the attack.

The crossbow remained clipped to Vicky's back. There seemed little point in using it at that moment because the reload time would be too long. Instead, she swung her bat at the first creature to rush her. A wet crack as it connected with the diseased's weak jaw and the thing fell to the ground. It disappeared beneath the stampede as its brethren surged forward.

Some of the other people from Home grunted as they too swung for the diseased. The sound mixed with the screams of the monsters receiving the blows.

As much as Vicky wanted to check on the other guards—Flynn especially—the diseased came at them too quickly for her to focus on anything else.

Swing after swing and the monsters fell away from Vicky, some of them screaming as they went down, while others fell without a sound, clearly knocked out from the blow. The soundless remained down while the noisier ones rolled around as if fighting to get back up again.

Sweat ran into Vicky's eyes, the warmth of the June day still in the air despite the fading sun. The stench of the diseased around her seemed worse for the summer heat, but Vicky gulped against her desire to heave and pushed on.

"Someone make sure they're dead," Vicky called out, the vibration of another blow running up her baseball bat into her shoulders. "Clean up behind us. Stab the fuckers in the head. We don't want to get caught out here."

Whether someone heard her or not, she couldn't tell, but she hoped they did.

A moment's respite and Vicky looked back over her shoulder to see the people of Home were winning. Maybe they did have it in them. The sight sent a surge of adrenaline through her and she found the impetus to carry on.

Ten, twelve, fifteen ... each blow scored a direct hit, and, with Vicky's expertise, she silenced more than she didn't. An ache gripped her jaw from clenching it tightly, but she kept going. Blow after blow after blow.

A glance to her right and Vicky expected to see Serj or Piotr or Flynn leading the attack with her. Instead, she saw Sally—the meek and mild woman that Hugh had wanted to evict for being useless. She looked to be possessed. Wild eyes and a fierce scowl, she matched Vicky strike for strike. Together they tore a hole into the diseased's ranks.

When Sally looked across, Vicky nodded at her and she nodded back, her face covered in the blood of the fallen.

The crowd of diseased bodies thinned from the onslaught, many of them lying in the long grass and not getting back up again. Soon they'd have to face the people from Moira's community—if they were still there. Vicky called out, "We're doing this. Keep it up, guys."

A cry sounded out to Vicky's right and she looked across through the mess of bodies. She saw a gang of people she presumed to have been the ones attacking the solar panels. They'd grabbed Stuart and two others and had them outnumbered at least three to one.

"Fuck it," Vicky said and turned to Sally. She then saw Serj, Flynn, and Piotr had appeared next to her. "Keep fighting," she called to all of them. "I'll be back in a second."

Flynn stared at Vicky, the blood of the diseased dripping from his sweating face, and he looked like he wanted to say something. But she spoke before he could. "Stay there! I'll be back soon, I promise."

A shake of his head and Flynn continued to fight. He clearly didn't want to stay there, but he listened to her nonetheless.

Vicky fought against her exhaustion as she shimmied and weaved through the throng of fighting bodies after Stuart and the other two. They wouldn't get taken. Not on her watch.

Chapter Forty-Eight

Once Vicky got free from the fighting, she had a clearer sight of the people who'd dragged Stuart and the other two away. About ten in total—less than she'd seen smashing up the solar panels—they had a head start on her, and by the time she reached the bottom of the hill with Home's front door in it, they were disappearing over the top of it.

Vicky was sweating from her fight with the diseased and now the chase. Her strength threatened to abandon her as she began the short but steep incline. She clenched her jaw and pushed on. At any moment her legs could stop working, but until then she'd give everything she had.

Darkness spread through the sky as night clenched its grip on the world, but when Vicky saw Stuart and the other two completely disappear over the brow of the hill, she found a burst of speed. She couldn't lose sight of them.

Vicky panted when she reached the top and looked over the field of solar panels—all the blacker for the darkening sky. Stuart and the others had vanished. Before she could catch her breath, the thick ropes of a heavy net crashed into her. They wrapped a tight embrace around her and she fell to the ground, rolling down the much smaller hill on the other side. A fly in a web, she came to rest at the bottom, completely entrapped in the cargo netting.

Only now did she see Stuart and the other two. They were gripped tightly by their captors. About twenty more guards stood with them and they all stared at Vicky on the ground.

It had been hard for Vicky to see at first, but now she'd gotten closer, she looked at what were two boys from Home. Both of them stood frozen, their eyes wide as they remained board stiff.

Stuart, on the other hand, twisted and turned as if he could get free from his captors.

When a woman no more than about five feet tall raised a bloody machete to Stuart's face, the fight left him and he fell limp. She held the tip of the large blade close to his right eyeball and snarled at him.

Stuart looked at Vicky and said, "I'm so sorry."

The more Vicky moved, the tighter she found herself trapped within the twisted net. She shook her head at him. "Don't be. There's nothing you can do to help."

Before Stuart could say anything else, one of the men from Moira's community linked both of his hands together and drove them into his stomach.

With a loud *oomph*, Stuart bent over double and he fell to the ground in a heap.

Although he looked like he wanted to speak as he stared at Vicky through wide and watering eyes, he had to fight too hard for breath to get his words out. He looked like a fish as he lay there gasping.

Suddenly, Vicky's feet lifted a few inches from the ground and the rush of the long grass whooshed over the ropes as someone dragged her away through the solar panels. She looked at Stuart while the gap between them increased. He stared back and said nothing.

Until that moment, Vicky had shut it out, but as she got taken farther away from her community, the screams and shouts of the battle in front of Home came to her.

When Vicky had got about twenty metres away, Stuart seemed to finally find enough oxygen to call after her. "I'll come for you, Vicky. I'll save you, tr—*oomph*." He must have taken another blow.

The gesture seemed like a sweet one, but the guy didn't have a clue. Now that Vicky had escaped from Moira's community once, she'd punish her so quickly she wouldn't be able to do it again. Hell, she wouldn't be able to do anything again. She'd be in that pit the second they dragged her into the courtyard.

"You won't get away with this, you know," Vicky called to the figures who dragged her away. With so much netting around her, she couldn't make out any more than their silhouettes. "My friends will come for me and burn your community to the ground. You'll *pay* for this."

The people stopped dragging Vicky, and one of them snarled, "Shut up, you cunt."

Vicky saw the foot a second before it sent a white flash through her vision. The copper taste of her blood flooded her mouth and her world turned dark.

Chapter Forty-Nine

When Vicky came to, her headache sat in her eyeballs and drove pain through them as if they were glass about to shatter. Unable to see much because of her heavy squint, she lay on cold concrete and smelled the heady reek of piss and shit. The fear-laden silence told her exactly where they'd taken her—not that she had to be a genius to work it out.

Vicky groaned and rolled over. Free of the netting at least, her face throbbed from having been kicked and the swelling added extra weight to her mouth and cheeks. She could still taste blood.

Despite the very clear reek of the place and the sound of movement around her, Vicky saw nothing. Repeated blinks went some way to clearing her vision. They must have kicked her straight in the eyes.

"And she's *finally* awake!"

A look in the direction of the sound and Vicky sneered. It didn't matter that she couldn't see, she knew that voice all too well.

The raking rasp of her tone was like fingernails down a

chalkboard. "Moan all you like, love. It won't do you much good. We've even told your community we have no interest in a war with them now. We have what we want. Bygones and all that."

Vicky's vision finally cleared. Still dark from the night sky above, she looked around at the same small cell she'd been trapped in before. A few metres square, it had a frigid concrete ground and chain-link fence walls.

Nausea flipped through Vicky's guts when she sat upright and her head spun. When she opened and closed her jaw, electric pain streaked through it. Whoever kicked her had put their full force into it.

Vicky looked at Moira. Scraggly black hair, sagging skin, a hooked nose. A broomstick and a black cat would have topped off the image.

The prisoners remained in the larger cage next to Vicky. All of them sat together as if seeking warmth from one another, and all of them looked prisoner-of-war thin. After a quick scan of them, Vicky's heart racing because she couldn't see him, she finally laid eyes on Aaron. He stared back at her from the large orbs in his withdrawn face. Dark rings hung beneath his eyes. His skin pulled so tightly across his skull it formed a paper-thin layer over the bone.

"Although," Moira said, pulling Vicky's attention back to her, "I still quite like the look of your place. *Home*? Is that what you call it?"

"You think we hadn't worked that out?"

"Oh?"

"If you didn't want it, you would have done the one thing

that would have flushed us out instantly."

"Destroy the solar panels?" Moira said and, before Vicky could answer, added, "You're a *smart* one, aren't you?"

"It doesn't take a genius."

"Well, you're right. Smashing those things would have been like sending smoke into a bees' nest. We'd have flushed you out in minutes."

"But then you wouldn't be able to use them for yourself."

A crooked smile spread across Moira's face. "And you know the best part?"

"I'm sure you're going to tell me."

"They *genuinely* believe we won't attack them now."

Before Vicky could respond, Moira said, "I know what you're thinking."

"You do?"

"That we'll still attack Home, and that the people of Home will be ready for us. But I think we've already proven we're smarter than you are."

Vicky forgot her pains momentarily and ground her jaw. She winced at the sting of it and the pound of her headache ran harder through her vision. "What's with the bullshit monologue, Moira? What are you? A fucking James Bond villain? Or do you just like the sound of your own voice?"

The reaction seemed to please Moira more than anything Vicky had said so far and she let out a titter of a laugh. "Surely you need to allow me my moment? We've meticulously planned this, and the best part is revealing it to you. It's like thinking really hard about a Christmas present, buying it during the summer months, and giving it to the one you love on Christmas

Day, when you've managed to keep the secret the entire time. Imagine what Flynn's face would be like had you done that."

Vicky didn't respond, her heart quickening at the mention of his name. It didn't belong in *her* mouth.

"We made you think we'd attack earlier. When you and your Indian friend were outside, a few of my people made sure you heard them talking about when we would do it."

A flashback to the moment when she and Serj had overheard the people from Moira's community made Vicky's stomach sink. She looked across at the prisoners next to her in the cage. How long would it be for her to look like that? For her to be so broken she existed as no more than a skeleton in a cell. Apathetic through exhaustion.

Glee lit up Moira's face when Vicky looked back at her again. It seemed hard to take anything the woman said at face value, but if the people from her complex hadn't known of Vicky and Serj's presence the other day, then Moira still wouldn't know of it now.

"You still don't believe me, eh?" Moira said. "We made sure you saw and heard us that night. We pretended we knew nothing about you being there. We wanted to force your hand. To expose you."

When Vicky scowled, it sent pain through her face, but she didn't say anything.

While she paced up and down outside Vicky's cell, Moira spread her arms wide in a theatrical display. "Then we let the diseased out of the pen. Nice idea, by the way; we should have thought of that one. Shame you held back though, eh? That could have worked really well if you'd had the balls to strike early.

"So even if your little gang do think they can outsmart us and get you back, I can assure you now, Victoria, they don't stand a fucking chance."

Although her legs shook from still feeling woozy, Vicky got to her feet and walked toward Moira. With clenched fists and a clenched jaw, she leaned against the cold chain-link fence and glared at the woman. A time would come when she could set her fury loose on her. When it did, she wouldn't hold back. She'd unload both barrels on the bitch.

After she'd tilted her head to the side and smiled wider than before, Moira said, "You want to say something to me, little one?"

Another look over at Aaron, and she saw the rage in his eyes too. Although, unlike Vicky, he directed his rage at her, not Moira. It robbed her of her fire and she sighed as she dropped her head and looked at the ground. She'd let a lot of people down. In fact, she'd let down everyone who currently trusted her in this life. Maybe she'd come to the end. Maybe that wouldn't be such a bad thing. At least Flynn had Piotr to look after him now.

Chapter Fifty

God knew how long Vicky dozed for; it couldn't have been very long. When she came to—not through any choice of her own, rather because of the rattling attack of Moira dragging something metal along the chain-link fence of her cell—the sky above still looked as dark as it had when she'd passed out. Nighttime for sure, but fuck knew what time of night.

The same twisted smile dominated Moira's haggard face. In one hand she had a metal baton—which she'd used to rattle the cage—and with her other hand, she pointed a finger at Vicky. On the end of her outstretched finger hung a key attached to a shoelace.

Vicky grabbed at her neck to find her key had gone. Of course it fucking had. They'd probably taken it before they'd locked her up.

"So—" Moira giggled, the shrill staccato of it sounding like someone on the precipice of madness "—not only does your group think they're safe from an attack from us, but we also have a way in whenever we choose to take it."

The community wouldn't lower their guard that easily.

Hopefully Serj had already replaced the locks. It must have got back to him that she'd been taken. Stuart would have told him. Vicky's heart kicked hard. Stuart probably hadn't survived. Although maybe they'd released him and the boys as a gesture of peace. They had Vicky; they didn't need anyone else. She couldn't think about it. The fact that she hadn't returned would be enough for Serj to change the locks. They only took longer with Meisha because they knew exactly where she and the key were.

Another bash against the cage, her baton exploding in a wash of sound that ran all around Vicky, and Moira said, "Anyway, I'm getting bored of this nonsense. You've served your purpose now, sweetheart, and I'm getting fed up of looking at your pathetic face. The longer I keep you around, the greater risk there is of you escaping again. It's happened once; trust me when I say it *won't* happen again."

One of Moira's guards walked to the padlock on Vicky's cell door, lifted the lock up, and slipped the key in.

Before he could walk to her, Vicky got to her feet, her hips and knees sore from lying on the hard and cold concrete.

A raised eyebrow and Moira watched Vicky stand still. "Not going to fight?"

"What's the point?" Vicky said as she stared at the vicious woman. "Will it achieve anything?"

"It may get you tied up." Moira raised her eyebrows again. "If that's your thing?"

The two women stared at one another for what felt like the longest time before Moira shrugged. "Fine. It's not like you'll survive anyway."

Vicky let the guard lead her from her cell into the forecourt. On her way out, she turned to the other prisoners. Aaron and the others stared at her, and for the first time in a while, he looked at her with something other than resentment. Pity, regret, condolences. They all knew what Moira would do with her now.

On the edge of starvation, Aaron had got so bony it probably hurt to sit on the cold concrete ground, yet he still pitied Vicky. No one wanted to go into the pit.

The guard had such a tight grip on her bicep, Vicky had to grit her teeth against the pain.

Wobbly on her legs as the guard dragged her, the scrape of metal over concrete called out as another one pulled the manhole cover free from the pit with the diseased in it. The call of the infected beasts below rang out into the cool night air.

The beginnings of a panic attack shifted in Vicky's chest as she walked. She breathed into her stomach to try to settle her frantic pulse. A headache still throbbed through her skull. The hole got closer with every step and bile lifted into her throat to look at it.

At the edge of the dark pit, Vicky peered in. Something moved in the shadows. A darker darkness shifting below her. But Vicky couldn't make out the form of it.

"It looks like this is the end for us, sweetheart," Moira said.

Aware of the guards moving in behind her, Vicky took control of her own destiny, drew one final breath—which had the tinge of diseased rot in it—and jumped in.

Chapter Fifty-One

The heat and stench of the pit hit Vicky before she hit the ground. The impact of landing ran a shock up her legs and sent shards of pain through her knees, but Vicky ignored it as best as she could and drew her knife from the back of her trousers.

Although dark in the pit, the moonlight did enough to give her an idea of what she faced. A space no larger than one of the bedrooms in Home, it had maybe fifteen to twenty diseased in it. No doubt a few more since the family had been dropped in there.

When one of the diseased came at her, Vicky swiped at it with her knife and caught the beast's arm. It roared and withdrew.

Vicky couldn't prevent herself from heaving at the stench of the pit, the hot cloying air drying her throat and lining the back of her tongue with a stale taste.

The sound of metal scraped over concrete above and the moonlight vanished. She needed a plan.

Now pitch black, Vicky took two steps backwards and found a wall. She then shifted to the side as the scream of a diseased rushed at her. It crashed into the space she'd occupied with a wet slap.

The diseased might have had numbers on their side, but they suffered with blindness just like Vicky did now the cover had been slipped across.

Hot and already gassed, Vicky did her best to calm her breathing down and listened to the sound of the beasts. Agitation clearly shimmered through them, but they didn't seem to have Vicky's location yet.

The clumsy steps moved closer to Vicky, who tightened her sweating grip on the handle of her knife and waited.

When one finally came close enough to her, she lunged.

A wet squelch as the knife stuck in the creature and it screamed in response. Not a fatal blow by any means.

The stench of the place seemed to wind up another level as the monster ran straight for her. This time Vicky lunged with the short blade. She aimed for head height and it worked. The knife sank into what felt like the thing's face. It turned instantly limp and Vicky withdrew her blade from it as it fell away. Before she had a moment to think, the next beast came at her.

Although the monsters descended on her, they couldn't find Vicky like they would have during the day.

Over the screams and rushing feet, Vicky did her best to hear the next approach. She located it and lunged forward again. Her blow met with a scream and the creature withdrew. She'd have to get better at this to survive.

The next blow delivered a popping squelch and turned another one flaccid.

Lunge after lunge after lunge. Some of them missed completely, and as Vicky pulled her hand back to reload for the next attack, she expected the sting of teeth to sink into her forearm.

Sweat ran into her eyes, she breathed heavily, and her head still pounded from the kick she'd taken to her face, but they hadn't got her yet.

The metallic reek of the creatures' blood changed the stench in the air and Vicky fought against her exhaustion to keep going. Someone had to lose. Hopefully it would be them.

Chapter Fifty-Two

Silence. Finally silence.

Well, not quite silence. Vicky's heavy breaths called through the hot, sweaty, and cramped space. But from what she could hear, the creatures didn't move—not a single one of them.

Not that Vicky trusted that.

Blind to the point where the darkness pushed in against her eyes, Vicky's only sense of the size of the pit came from the echoes of her sounds.

With her back against the rough dirt wall, Vicky's heart beat in her throat and she couldn't pull enough air into her body to recover. Despite her desire to move, she leaned back and tried to slow her breaths down.

Even now, after what she'd been through, Vicky shuddered to think of the bugs in the pit. A small army of diseased and she worried about creepy crawlies turning the dirt alive against her back. What a wuss! She shuddered and stepped forward a pace.

***

It took what felt like a few minutes for Vicky to recover. She held her breath for a second and listened. Still no sound. She had to trust she'd beaten them.

Cramps ran up Vicky's right arm from the fight. The grip she held on her blade made her knuckles ache, but she couldn't bring herself to sheathe her knife. If this world had taught her anything, it was that she should never drop her guard. Ever!

It would still be night outside. The battle might have seemed to last forever, but it couldn't have been any longer than ten minutes. Now would be Vicky's best chance to get the fuck out of there.

The ground in front of Vicky would be littered with bodies. When she kicked out, she made contact with one. It didn't move in response to her knock. It seemed like suicide, but she had to push forward. She put her knife in the back of her trousers and tried to find composure in the chaos swirling inside of her.

Vicky then reached down, grabbed the limp thing, and dragged it into what she guessed to be the middle of the pit. When she'd jumped into the hole, the moonlight gave her a snapshot of what the place looked like and she had to move based on that memory.

Vicky repeated the process with the next downed diseased, dragging it along and lying it over the limp body of the first one. Hopefully none of the fuckers would wake up. She shook her head. It would serve no purpose to think about it.

Each time Vicky kicked a monster to check for a reaction, and each time, when it didn't react, she dragged it back to the mounting pile of bodies.

By the time she'd dragged the fourth one over, she had to lift it because of the height of the pile in the middle. But she managed it, even with the aches in her exhausted body.

Sweat ran down Vicky's face again from the effort of moving the bodies in the hot hole. Every time she brought a new body to the pile, her confidence left her. Would this be the one she wouldn't be able to lift to the top?

Now eight bodies high, the floppy, stinking mess of death and rot would hopefully be high enough. Because she'd stacked them crossing over one another, two bodies making up an X, then two more bodies making the same shape, she hoped the structure would hold.

Vicky dropped her hands to her knees and pulled breaths so hard into her body, her back arched to the ceiling of the pit. As she faced the ground, she felt her sweat fall from her.

Once she'd recovered again, Vicky grabbed on to the stinking pile of flesh, drew one last breath, and boosted herself up as she started to climb.

***

Vicky had nothing to lean against other than the ceiling, so she scrabbled up the bodies as quickly as she could. She found purchase at some points and slipped at others, but she kept her forward momentum.

The manhole had been cut into thick concrete, so the metal circle of steel only took up a fraction of the hole. Vicky grabbed for the excess stone and caught the lip, which she used to steady herself.

The structure of bodies wobbled, and when a couple of them groaned, Vicky nearly jumped from the pile. But she heard nothing more. Before the world went to shit, she'd known an undertaker, and he'd told her how air leaving a body could make them groan. Despite the shake running through her, encouraging her to jump down, she stayed still. They were dead. The diseased didn't have the cunning to pretend not to be.

Another wobble as Vicky stood on tiptoes and reached up. The bodies still held. When she felt the cold metal of the manhole cover, her nerves settled a little. One final deep breath and she pushed against it.

Chapter Fifty-Three

Although dark outside, the moonlight shone a torch into the void Vicky had existed in. Now had to be the best time to escape. Hopefully the guards would be asleep or at least on the other side of the complex. After all, no one ever got out of the pit, so they probably wouldn't be watching it too closely.

Vicky lifted the manhole cover a little more and bit down on her bottom lip as she shifted it away as quietly as she could manage. Once she'd moved it clear enough, she lowered it, her hips moving and tilting as she rode out the wobble from the stack of cadavers.

When Vicky poked her head out of the hole, she looked at the alleyway leading to the guards' accommodation. It seemed clear. She then looked over at the large cage. Every prisoner in there stared back at her. She made eye contact with Aaron and spun her index finger in a circle to indicate her surroundings. "Is it clear?"

The bug-eyed and emaciated Aaron nodded yes.

Vicky nodded back, bent her tired legs, and pushed off against the stack of corpses. The top body slipped as she forced herself away from it, but Vicky managed to hook her elbows against the top side of the concrete hole and pulled herself to the surface, the rough ground biting through the thin fabric of her shirt.

A wet *thud* and Vicky looked down to see the pile of bodies had come apart and spread out on the ground like a cake unable to hold its shape.

Now she peered into the hole at the mess beneath her, Vicky shook worse than before. How the fuck had she managed to survive down there?

A hiss from the cage pulled Vicky's attention over to it and she saw Aaron, his eyes even wider.

One final look into the pit and Vicky saw the small figure with army gear on. The youngest of the family. A pain ran through her chest to see the glistening hole in the centre of the girl's face. Poor kid. Although, like Meisha—hell, like anyone—once they'd been bitten, they were gone. She hadn't stabbed a little girl, she'd stabbed a stinking diseased.

The prisoners were silent as they watched on, all of them leaning into the chain-link fence holding them back. They might not have said anything, but their body language told Vicky enough. *Hurry the fuck up!* She acknowledged them with a raised hand and scanned the area. It seemed to be free of guards.

Vicky then ran for the exit gate. A glance back at the prisoners in the cage and some of them seemed more agitated than before. They wouldn't let her run without a sound again. After all the empty promises she'd brought to them in the night, she had to take them with her this time; otherwise she wouldn't be going anywhere herself.

Vicky got to the rock she'd spied. It sat inside the complex, which saved her breaking out first. She lifted it from the ground and ran back over to the large cage. While moving, she raised the rock above her head and brought it down on the padlock with a heavy whack.

A loud *splash* of metal and the lock broke into pieces, tinkling against the hard ground as they fell. "Come *on*," Vicky hissed at the prisoners. "They'll be on us soon; we need to get the fuck out of here." She'd given them all she could, so she turned on her heel and headed for the main gate. Hopefully, the prisoners would follow.

The lock to the main gates gave way with one whack too and Vicky threw their exit wide open. When she looked behind, most of the prisoners had caught up to her and followed her out of the gates to the steep overgrown and lumpy hill leading away from Moira's complex.

Vicky wanted to run and leave them behind. She wanted to get back to Home and let the others fend for themselves, but she stood still at the open gates and waited for all of the prisoners to get out of the courtyard. She drew her knife, bounced on the spot to spend some of her impatience, and watched the alleyway for the appearance of guards.

Once every one of the weak prisoners had started their bid for freedom up the steep hill, Vicky followed them, taking up the rear and holding the slowest pace against every instinct in her exhausted body.

Chapter Fifty-Four

Impatience crawled over Vicky's skin as she followed the slow prisoners in their shuffle up the hill away from Moira's community. Step, stop. Step, stop. Step … If she had the strength, she would have pushed half the fuckers up herself.

Repeated glances behind and Vicky chewed the inside of her mouth after each step up the hill. It didn't look like any of the guards had come to investigate the sounds of their escape. But then again, the night cast such a deep shadow over the complex, they could be hiding in it without her being any the wiser.

Step, stop. Step, stop. When a particularly slow man nearly halted in front of her, Vicky gave in and shoved his bony bottom. "Come on, mate. You need to keep moving. You can rest when we get to Home."

He responded by taking his next step. A tortoise of a man, he slowly edged away from Moira's community.

Not even halfway up the hill, Vicky saw some of the front runners crest it and disappear from view. Aaron seemed to be among them. At least one of them knew where to go.

Vicky's head spun from how many times she looked behind

to check the complex and then looked back up the hill again. Every time she checked, it still seemed clear. Surely Moira's lot would be on their tail by now if they were going to chase them.

Another nudge to the man in front of her and Vicky watched more of the group reach the top of the hill before she looked to her left and right. For all the diseased that had been outside of Home, it seemed clear.

***

Once the slow man reached the top of the hill, Vicky did one final check behind. Still no movement. How the fuck they'd got this far without being caught, she didn't know. Although, knowing Moira, the woman probably had a trap set for them somewhere. Make them feel like they'd got away and then fuck them over moments before freedom.

Far enough out of earshot, Vicky clapped her hands at the group and said, "Well done on getting up the hill, guys, you've dealt with the hardest part now. It's either flat or downhill all the way to Home from here."

It seemed like most, if not all, of the prisoners had waited for Vicky at the top of the hill. A quick check and she saw Aaron among them. "Can you lead the front-runners?" she asked him.

The darkness had turned his sunken eyes into two shadowed holes, and the silver highlights from the moon lit up his cheekbones. The shine on his face moved up and down when he nodded.

When the group set off again, Vicky remained on the brow of the hill with half of her attention down below. As she waited, she tapped her hands against her thighs and bounced on the spot again. Her heart beat with such a fierce kick, it rocked her where she stood.

Only when the slowest of the group had nearly gone from sight did Vicky follow them.

***

After a slow walk through the solar panels with the same man she'd followed up the hill, Vicky pulled his left arm around her shoulder and helped him down the short, steep drop leading to Home's front door. The guy stank of the prison: rotten food and human waste. But she turned her face away from him as they descended and held her breath.

At the bottom, Vicky slipped from underneath him and nodded at the man. He nodded back. They were both okay.

The crowd parted to give Vicky a clear path to the front door. Keyless, she had to knock on the large wooden barrier. She made a fist and bashed the side of it against the door, sending a loud *boom* out across the landscape behind her. Another look into the dark and it still seemed free of the diseased.

When no one responded, Vicky called out, "Let us in!" Her voice went the same way as her heavy knock. Still no diseased.

Whether still Friday night or the early hours of Saturday morning, there wouldn't be anyone in the canteen. Vicky stepped back and looked up at the white security camera above Home's entrance. While waving her arms above her head, she jumped up and down on the spot. "It's Vicky, guys. Let me in."

For all the people around her, they stood as quiet as ghosts and Vicky paused again to listen for the murmur of the diseased in the distance. Nothing.

Just before Vicky could knock again, the click of the lock on the other side of the door snapped free.

A crack opened in the door, and when Vicky saw Serj's face, her legs buckled beneath her.

"You're back," Serj said as he rushed out and helped get Vicky to her feet.

Not one for outward displays of emotion, Vicky hugged Serj when he pulled her up, the lump in her throat so large she could barely breathe.

When they pulled away from one another, Vicky managed to stand on her own. "Get everyone to the canteen," she said. "We need a meeting now."

A half smile lifted Serj's face.

"What?" Vicky asked.

"All you've been through and you're still thinking about the community."

"I'm afraid we have to. If we don't take care of Moira now, we're fucked."

Chapter Fifty-Five

Within just a few minutes, the first of Home's residents stumbled into the canteen. Bed hair, bleary eyes, and walking as if they were the diseased, they shuffled into the space. Many of them found seats at tables and waited.

When Sally appeared, Vicky—who stood with the prisoners she'd rescued from Moira's community—walked over to her. "Sally, can you take these people, please? They need to eat and get cleaned up."

Pity twisted Sally's features to look at the group. She then turned her attention to Vicky and nodded. "Sure."

"Right, guys," Vicky said, her voice echoing through the canteen, making some of the newly awakened arrivals flinch at the loudness of it, "if you follow Sally, she'll look after you. She'll get you some food, a shower, and some clean clothes." For the first time, Vicky looked at the prisoners without guilt. A ragtag bunch of both men and women, their ages ranged from about twenty to about sixty. No children. It didn't bear thinking about where they'd gone.

Sally moved off and the slow trudge of broken prisoners

followed her. Although Vicky watched them, she also glanced at the monitors on the wall of the canteen. They showed the darkness of outside, but still not a single diseased. When a man walked near her, Vicky grabbed his arm as she said, "Excuse me, what happened to all the diseased?"

Only when she took a proper look at the man did she recognise him. Brian, the one who seemed to have more of a hatred for Vicky than even Sharon or Dan. For a moment he scowled at her.

"Look, Brian," Vicky said. "It's been a long fucking night, so spare me your bullshit and just answer my fucking question, yeah?"

Clearly caught off guard by her comment, Brian's face flushed red. "We killed them all when we were outside the community. Not that *you* were any help."

Although Vicky drew a breath to respond, Brian walked off before she could. She clenched her fists as she watched his broad back.

The line of prisoners continued to file past and it took all Vicky had not to screw her nose up at their smell. Each one of them moved as if they had glass in their shoes. Each one of them looked on the edge of their balance.

When the back of the line filed through, Aaron appeared in front of Vicky. A skeleton grimace pulled on his face and it took a few seconds for her to recognise it as a smile. "Thank you," he said, "I didn't think you'd be able to help us. I knew you wanted to, but I didn't think you had it in you. Thank you for proving me wrong. Thank you for saving our lives. We won't forget it." He leaned forward and wrapped Vicky in a bony hug.

The marked change from Brian's aggression to Aaron's gratitude sent Vicky's head spinning and she squeezed his slight frame. "You're welcome. Now, go and get yourself healthy again. We're going to need your farming skills to keep this place running."

To see the glisten of tears in Aaron's eyes made Vicky's eyes itch too and her view of him blurred. After she'd cleared her throat, she said, "Go *on*, don't make me look weak in front of this lot."

"It's a *strength* that you care." Aaron squeezed her hands. "Don't fool yourself into thinking of it as anything else."

Vicky said nothing more and watched the man walk away.

Chapter Fifty-Six

Maybe all of the people had turned up or maybe just most of them. Like when they went out to fight against the diseased earlier that day, Vicky couldn't give it too much thought. A mostly full canteen, she couldn't leave them too long at this time of night because they'd understandably lose interest.

Vicky made her way through the packed tables—the level of chatter rising with each passing minute—and headed for the blue crash mats on the other side of the hall.

Before Vicky got there, Stuart stood up in front of her. His blue eyes sparkled and a wide grin spread across his face. "Vicky!" he said, reaching forward and holding both of her hands. "I'm so glad you're okay. I was worried about you."

Not one for close contact, Vicky cringed as she endured the second hug in the past few minutes. She offered Stuart a tight-lipped smile as they pulled away from one another. Her interaction with Brian still left a bitter taste in her mouth. In some small way, Stuart's kindness helped dilute that.

When Vicky got to the front of the room, the chatter died down and the people looked at her. Flynn, Piotr, and Serj already waited and all three of them nodded at her when she stood beside them. Flynn gave her the most tight-lipped response of the three.

Vicky drew a breath and opened her mouth to speak, but Sharon cut her off. On one of the closest tables to the front, she sat there with her husband, Dan. Brian had also joined them. "Before you start," the mum of the dead children sneered, "I want to know what you've brought into this community."

The question disarmed Vicky and she opened and closed her mouth a couple of times before she said, "I beg your pardon?" her response echoing through the large space.

"Those *things*!" Sharon said as she straightened her back in her seat.

"Moira's prisoners, you mean?"

"*Things!*"

A calming breath did nothing to bring Vicky's rising fury under control. "You do realise you're talking about *people*, right?"

"They're also *all* men!"

"No, they're *not*, you moron. At least half of them are women."

When Sharon didn't respond, Vicky threw her arms up in the air. "So what's your point? Come on, love, spit it out."

"My point is they come into this community disguised as prisoners, but they could be working for Moira for all we know. They could be moving in under the guise of needing help and bring us down from the inside."

A couple of people other than Dan and Brian nodded at Sharon's words, but only a couple. The rest of the community seemed uncomfortable with the conversation, shifting on their seats and staring at the floor.

Instead of responding to the woman, Vicky looked at the people of Home. "So I've been in Moira's community again."

"You haven't asked anyone's permission to bring them here," Sharon said, cutting her off.

"Have you *seen* them?"

Sharon didn't reply.

"Go and look at the state of them. Look at how skinny they are. They're wasting away. Quite an extreme length to go to, to slip into our community, wouldn't you say? Most of them can't even walk properly they're so malnourished. I struggle to see how anyone would do that to get inside a community that Moira's going to attack anyway."

A lingering stare at Sharon and she didn't respond, so Vicky looked at the other people. "We always knew this day would come, and it's been getting closer. We need to go to war *tomorrow.*"

"But you didn't ask anyone's permission," Sharon said.

Fire rushed through Vicky and her pulse pounded when she roared, "Fucking hell, Sharon! I get that you're upset, I really do. And you have every right to be. It's fucking shit what's happened to your family. But *I* didn't do it—"

"Everything was fine before you turned up."

"But it *wasn't*, that's the point. How many fucking times, Sharon? Moira still planned on taking you down, you just didn't know about it. This day was *always* going to come."

"You still haven't asked permission to take the prisoners in."

"Serj," Vicky said with a sigh as she turned to the leader of Home.

Serj flicked his head up at her.

"You okay with the prisoners being here?"

Serj nodded.

Vicky looked at Sharon, Dan, and Brian. Sharon opened her mouth to respond, and Vicky cut her off, "Grind your axe another day, Sharon. We have *serious* issues to deal with here."

Another inhale as if she would go for Vicky again, but Sharon remained quiet.

After she'd watched Sharon for a few seconds, Vicky turned to the group. Half of them stared at her with their mouths wide open.

"As I said a moment ago, Moira's coming. We need to take this fight to her. We need to end this war now. She may have told you she wouldn't come here if she had me, but she didn't mean it."

A sea of confused faces looked at Vicky, who turned to Serj. "You *didn't* have a conversation with Moira?"

"I would have slit her throat had she come anywhere near me."

Dan spoke from the dissenting group this time. "So Moira was happy with just you? She would have left us alone if you'd stayed there? *Again?*"

Vicky sighed, but it did little to dilute her rage. "*No!* That's my *point*. She's coming to attack regardless of what she says and we need to deal with it. If I'd have stayed in her complex, you wouldn't even have this warning."

"Convenient," Brian said.

Vicky ignored him. She then said, "Other than the prisoners—who are too weak to fight—we *all* need to be ready for this."

"You're going to leave them in *here?*" Sharon said.

"Now go and get some rest," Vicky said to the group. "You're going to need it. First thing in the morning we're going to war."

A lot of pale faces and sombre nods responded to Vicky's address. Hardly inspiring, but the facts were far from inspiring. They had a war to fight and it would be on their doorstep before they knew it.

Exhausted from the day and night, Vicky watched the slow shuffle of people as they left the room to go back to their sleeping quarters.

Dan, Sharon, and Brian remained where they were. When Vicky walked past them, Sharon said, "This is all your fault."

Before Vicky could think, she'd jumped on top of Sharon and pinned her to the ground by her throat. She watched the woman's mouth flap and her face turn red. She squeezed harder as she clenched her jaw. Although she felt what she assumed to be Dan and Brian pulling at her, Vicky didn't let go. "You think this is *easy* for me?" she said as she dribbled on the woman through her gritted teeth. "You think I like seeing people die? You think I like taking responsibility for useless fucks like *you*?"

But Sharon couldn't reply. Instead, she turned redder and the veins on her temples bulged.

It took for two large arms to wrap around Vicky and yank to get her off Sharon.

The two women stared at one another while Piotr kept a hold of Vicky.

Sharon stroked her neck where she'd been choked and her eyes streamed with tears. Although Vicky expected her to say something, she simply shook her head, spun on her heel, and walked away.

Chapter Fifty-Seven

Piotr only relaxed his constrictor grip on Vicky after Sharon, Dan, and Brian had left the canteen. Not that she would have followed them, but Piotr had a duty to keep the peace in Home. Besides, she'd done some pretty flighty things in the past few weeks, so maybe he'd made a good judgment call.

After the large Russian and Serj had also left the canteen, Vicky looked at Flynn. Only two of them in the room now, she said, "Shouldn't you be getting some rest?" She glanced at the monitors, which only showed how dark it was outside.

The acoustics in the large room sounded very different now all the people had left it, and Flynn's voice echoed when he said, "You should have taken me with you when you went to save Stuart and the other two."

Despite watching him grow up and change, Vicky still hadn't got used to Flynn's manly voice. "You were fighting the diseased, Flynn. I couldn't take you away from that."

"But it was so *clearly* a trap. I could have helped you. You could have been *killed*."

"But I wasn't, was I?"

"But you *could* have been. You're so fucking selfish, Vicky. You need to think about people other than yourself."

"I do," Vicky said. "That's why I won't take you with me."

"You need to stop protecting me. I'm not a child."

How many times would she have to argue with him about the same fucking thing? Maybe she just needed to be a lot more direct. "You're *sixteen*, Flynn, not thirty-five. You wouldn't even be old enough to drink in the old world. Or buy e-cigarettes. Stop being such a self-righteous little brat and appreciate what we're doing for you to keep you safe in this fucked-up world."

Flynn pursed his lips and Vicky watched his nostrils flare as she listened to his heavy breaths.

Before he could say anything, Vicky said, "Besides, you say you can look after yourself, but you twisted your ankle and needed help the last time we were out."

"Not the last time."

"Before that you made a noise that revealed us to the diseased. That was what brought the crowd of them down on Home in the first place."

"The crowd that you and Serj collected, you mean?"

Vicky glared at him.

"This world wouldn't be fucked up were it not for you. You walk around as if you're the boss, but the virus never would have left the Alpha Tower if you hadn't helped the terrorists. How do you think everyone else would feel to know this mess is all *your* fault? You only have to look after me because *you* created this!"

Vicky balled her fists as she stared at the boy. He had no idea what she'd been through. Like she didn't blame herself for everything that happened with Brendan, Oscar, or whatever the fuck his real name was.

Instead of attacking Flynn, Vicky turned her back on him and headed for the exit of the canteen. When she saw Piotr standing there, a confused frown on his broad face as he looked straight at her, she froze.

They stared at one another and it seemed to last an age before Piotr shook his head at Vicky and walked away.

Vicky's shoulders slumped with a deep sigh and she muttered, "Fuck it."

Chapter Fifty-Eight

Vicky walked toward the canteen the next morning, numb with exhaustion. How could anyone expect her to lead the war against Moira? The only time she'd had to stay awake over the past few weeks, she'd slept like a baby, and now she couldn't buy a good night's sleep.

Dread sat in Vicky's stomach as a dead weight. The anticipation of war tore at her guts, but to know Piotr had heard Flynn's accusations the previous night turned the thumbscrews on her anxiety. As much as she'd wanted to pretend to herself he hadn't heard it, he had. Of course he fucking had.

And what if he'd told someone already? The disgust she'd seen on his face showed exactly what he thought of Vicky, but would he keep it to himself? What if he told the wrong person? Most of the residents hated her, or at least feared her; it wouldn't do well for them to know she'd been responsible for forcing them all underground in the first place. Their loved ones had died because of her.

First to arrive in the canteen, Vicky saw the daylight from the windows in the foyer spill down the stairs. The smell of boiled cabbage hit her as it always did. When she looked at the monitors, her stomach flipped and she stopped dead.

The view outside showed a risen sun over the meadow in front of Home. It also showed something else. At the very edge of where Vicky could see stood a line of people. Men, women, and even teenagers. Each of them appeared to have a weapon of some sort. Bats, bars, chains, a few swords. They all faced Home, waiting patiently.

Maybe they'd been there all night. Maybe they'd only just arrived. Either way, they'd come for war, and Home needed to rise to the challenge.

Vicky spun around and returned to the corridor she'd just walked down. The corridor where she'd had to execute the diseased family just days ago. She yelled so loudly it burned her throat. "Get up now! They're here! Moira's community are here!"

The empty corridor amplified Vicky's voice. No one appeared, so she shouted again. "Hurry the fuck up! Moira's community are *outside*!"

When someone poked their head from a bedroom door, Vicky yelled, "Wake everyone up, *now*!"

A woman in her forties, she frowned at Vicky as if trying to decipher her words.

Although Vicky slowed her speech, she didn't lower the volume, a tickle in her throat from where she needed to cough. "Moira and her community are here. We need to mobilise *right now*."

The woman looked like she had more questions, but Vicky didn't give her the chance to ask them. Instead, she darted across the canteen to the corridor running parallel to the one she'd been in.

By the time Vicky got there, some of the people had already got up. Heavy breaths from the short run, she looked at the three or four faces and didn't know the name of a single one. Maybe they would have liked her more had she shown even a passing interest in them, but it was too late now. "We need to get ready," she called. "We're going to war!"

The spears the group had been making stood in a large bin in one corner of the canteen. Vicky jogged over to it and dragged it close to the stairs leading up to the front door of Home. The heavy barrel screeched along the hard linoleum floor.

At the sight of the first people emerging from the corridors, Vicky yelled, "Come on, get your weapons and get in the foyer. We need to face this."

Clearly still tired from being woke up, the first few people stumbled toward Vicky, but they watched the monitors as they moved along. A couple of them shook their heads at what they saw. All of them visibly woke up.

Vicky bounced on the balls of her feet. They weren't moving quick enough. If she had to, she'd go down there and drag the fuckers into the foyer. "We don't have time for this bullshit. They'll be on us before we know it if we don't do something now." With her pulse so frantic it felt as if her heart would burst, she said, "Hurry the fuck up!"

A young lad, who looked to be about eighteen at the most, continued to watch the screen as he said, "Can't we wait for the diseased to get them?"

"Have you seen how many of them are out there? They'll

take down even the biggest herd of the fuckers and then they'll descend on this place. We need to meet them out in the middle of the field where we can fight them."

Another look at the monitors again and Vicky saw an old oil barrel with flames stretching from it. "What if they set fire to this place with us in it? We're sitting ducks in here."

The boy seemed far from keen, but from the stoicism on his face, Vicky saw he clearly understood where she came from. Pulled back shoulders and a raised chin, the boy walked over to her, his pale skin turning paler with every second.

Vicky offered him a spear and he took it before he walked up the stairs into the foyer. She patted his shoulder on his way past. "Good work. Now wait there until we're all ready to go. We can win this. We can outfight them." Even as she said the words, her resolve faltered. Hopefully, if Moira's lot were as useless as the people of Home, they might stand a chance.

Tight-lipped and a clenched jaw, the boy nodded as he continued up. How many of them would have to die today?

Chapter Fifty-Nine

Not one for head counts, Vicky scanned the foyer and gauged most of Home to be there now. Even if some had stayed behind, they had to get out into the meadow before Moira's lot came for them. Stuart had given the rest of the spears out while Vicky went to the armoury and picked up a crossbow and baseball bat. Those who had taken weapons out to fight the diseased the previous day still had them. For those who didn't, the spears would have to do.

As she shuffled through the press of bodies in the foyer, Vicky ruffled her nose in response to the acrid reek of sick. Nerves had clearly got to some. By the smell of things, nerves had clearly got to quite a few of them. But they'd made it up there and they remained there. When it came to the battle, they'd forget their nausea and defend their lives. Besides, better to get it out now.

At the front of the foyer—the two large windows and door between her and the people from Moira's community—Vicky walked up and down in front of the crowd. Serj stood on one side of her, Piotr and Flynn on the other. Maybe she imagined it, but when she looked at Piotr, she met his dark stare in response. It wouldn't serve any purpose to think about it now.

"This is it," Vicky said to the group. "We win this war and we get peace. We wait in here and they'll flush us out like rats. We need to take the fight to them. Are you ready?"

Silence.

After a deep breath to settle her roiling stomach, Vicky shouted so loud it burned her throat. "I said are you ready for this?"

Flynn, Serj, Sally, and Stuart all shouted, "Yeah!" Their combined voices had quite an effect in the cramped space and the almost still group of people moved and shifted. Piotr continued to glare at Vicky.

As she pumped her fist in the air, Vicky called again, "Are you *ready* for this?"

"Yeah!" A few more people joined in.

Piotr didn't. Brian, Sharon, and Dan didn't.

They didn't matter right now. "Are you *ready* for this?"

"Yeah!"

"Are you *ready* for this?"

"YEAH!"

Vicky walked up to Brian and leaned in his face as she screamed so loudly her head spun, "ARE YOU *READY* FOR THIS?"

"YEAH!" the group called, but Brian still didn't respond, his lips pursed, his jaw clenched, his eyes narrowed.

Fuck Brian. Vicky cracked the two bolts on the front door free and pulled it wide. The fresh morning breeze rushed into the place, blowing away the stench of sick. The long grass swayed in front of them. It moved more than the line of people waiting to fight them.

After she'd stared at the people on the other side of the meadow, adrenaline searing through her, Vicky drew a deep breath that lifted her chest and called out at them, "Let's fucking have them, then!"

The people behind her screamed and yelled as Vicky led the charge.

Chapter Sixty

Adrenaline forced Vicky's tiredness from her as she released a battle cry. Her community behind her matched it with equal ferocity.

Although when Moira's army answered with their own call, Vicky nearly ground to a halt. The wall of sound damn near blew her hair back. But if she stopped at that moment, how could she expect the people behind her to keep going? They were committed now, and as their leader, she needed to fucking lead.

The long grass pulled against Vicky's progress. Not that she could give it any more than a passing thought, her attention returning to the army in front of her.

It had been dark and Vicky had been on the receiving end of a beating when she'd been in Moira's community the couple of times she'd been captured by them. So other than Moira, she didn't recognise any of the wild faces now rushing at them. Men, women, and teenagers, not a single one looked familiar.

Regardless of who they used to be, they all came at Vicky and the community of Home with just one intent. If they were to survive this, Home needed to match that intent.

Vicky roared again, freed her crossbow from her back and raised it as she ran. The stamp of feet shook the ground around her.

The bow kicked when Vicky set the first bolt free and she watched it sink into the face of a boy no more than about fourteen. It took the scream from him before he could loose it and he fell backwards into the long grass.

Another bolt loaded and ready to go, Vicky set it loose again. The *whoosh* of it rushed through the air and landed in the chest of a man with a *thump* as if it had just sunk into a tree. Over six feet tall, the man went down hard, tripping a couple of the people around him. The stampede from their own side ran over all three of them.

One final bolt and one final casualty. Another man, he went down like the other two had. Vicky didn't have time to load a fourth bolt. Instead, she threw the crossbow at the woman in front of her and followed it up with a swing of her bat.

The bat connected on the top of the woman's head with a deep *tonk* and the woman's legs folded beneath her. Dead or just unconscious, as long as the woman had fallen, Vicky didn't care.

A man filled the space the woman had occupied and Vicky swung for him. She landed another blow and dropped another person.

Aware of the fighting around her, Vicky kept her attention on the people in front. To think about everyone on the battlefield would spin her out. She could only focus on those she had to fight.

A hard contact crashed into Vicky's left shoulder and she

stumbled sideways. She clattered into a woman from Home, who raised her spear, her eyes wide and her nostrils flared. The mask of fury quickly cleared, pushed aside by comprehension as the woman clearly realised who Vicky was. She turned her spear on the man in front of her from Moira's community and drove it—with two hands—into his chest.

Whatever hit Vicky's left arm had turned it dead. Being right-handed gave her the dexterity to jab her bat into the face of the person in front of her. A slight girl no older than about sixteen, she took the end of the baseball bat to her nose with a wet *crunch* and fell backwards.

Vicky's heart ached along with her exhausted and beaten body to see the girl go down. So few humans left on the planet and they could only manage to fight one another.

Until that moment, Vicky hadn't noticed Brian, Dan, and Sharon fighting on the left of her. They stabbed and kicked, blood coating the shafts of their spears and spraying their clothes. The metallic reek of it mixed with the sweaty, shitty stench of battle.

When Vicky looked back in front, three of Moira's guards homed in on her. Maybe Moira had earmarked her as a target before they started. No, Moira had definitely earmarked her as a target. The three large men looked to be carrying out orders as they closed in. Two of them had machetes while the third had a bent crowbar.

Vicky's already ragged heart leapt higher in her throat as if trying to escape her body. No matter how she tried to drag breaths into her lungs, she couldn't get the oxygen she needed. A look at Brian and the others and they all looked back at Vicky first and then the men closing in on her. As one, the three of them turned away.

"What the fuck?" Vicky yelled, but she didn't have time to protest any further because the three men had slowed down and formed a semicircle around her.

Shallow of breath and with a dry throat, Vicky stepped back a pace. A fox cornered by wolves, she looked from one of the men to the other, each one of them ravenous with intent. They were here to destroy her. The people who could have helped her had just turned their backs.

A quick glance to her right and Vicky saw the woman with the spear next to her locked in a battle with a teenage boy. The boy had a sword, the sunlight glinting off the blade as he lunged forward with it. The woman next to her bent over double—her mouth stretched wide—and she folded into the long grass.

When Vicky looked back at the men closing in on her, she shook beyond her control. She looked left at Brian, Dan, and Sharon again and saw they'd moved farther away from her than before.

Vicky refocused on the men. If she had to go down, she needed to take at least one of them with her. After tightening her grip on her bat, she shook her head to herself and stepped forward to her death.

Chapter Sixty-One

A flash of a person appeared in Vicky's right peripheral vision and she jumped back to avoid them.

Stuart—spear in hand—lunged at one of the two with a machete and he drove the tip of his spear into the man's face. It sank into him with a wet *schlop,* and Stuart quickly withdrew the spear as the man fell into the long grass.

Before Stuart could launch another attack, the second man with a machete brought it through the air in a wide arc that culminated in the middle of Stuart's crown.

Blood sprayed Vicky's face and she flinched away. As Stuart fell, she dodged to the side to get out of his way. Her stomach dropped to see him down and the world blurred in front of her as tears stretched across her eyes. But she didn't have time to cry. Not now. Instead, she stepped over the fallen Stuart and swung her bat at the man who'd attacked him. A vibration pinged up the bat and the man fell.

Before the final man of the three could respond, Vicky took him down too. She threw repeated blows at his head when he hit the ground, turning his skull to a pulp in the long grass.

The fight continued around Vicky, and she couldn't gauge which side had the advantage. Although at that moment it stopped mattering. The sound lit up the air and rang louder than any battle cry.

More than one of them, it came from behind Moira's gang.

The call of the diseased.

Chapter Sixty-Two

No matter how many times Vicky heard it, the call of the diseased lit up her spine with an electric chill. She squinted to look at the rising sun on the horizon, and although too many of Moira's community stood between her and the diseased for her to get a true idea of their numbers, the sound and the frantic blur of the scuffle at the back of the meadow indicated there were enough to keep Moira's lot busy.

Other than the front line, Moira's guards turned their backs on the fight with Home and focused on the diseased. A preconditioned response to a formidable enemy, they'd just left themselves at the mercy of Home.

Those from Home who managed to keep their heads took advantage of the turned backs and a score or more of Moira's guards were quickly knocked down.

Before they could attack again, Vicky called out, "Retreat! Get back to Home now. Let *them* fight the diseased. This battle is over for us."

A few people from Home, rocking with their ragged breaths and covered in the blood of their enemy, stopped and looked at

Vicky. But when they saw the others turn and run back, they took off after them.

Even before the first person reached Home's open door, Vicky heard the sounds of the battle between Moira's lot and the diseased get louder. Snarls and growls collided with screams and cries.

Not the first to Home's front door, but among the first and after Flynn, Vicky stood in the doorway and watched the residents return. Maybe she wouldn't recognise if some of Moira's crowd tried to sneak in, but between her and Flynn, they would hopefully pick them out.

Covered in blood, limping, and just plain exhausted, the people funnelled back into the complex. A mixture of pain and relief painted their faces. Because Moira's lot separated them and the diseased, Vicky didn't worry about any of them having been bitten and let them all in.

When Brian, Dan, and Sharon approached, Vicky clenched her jaw and balled her fists. "Stuart *died* because of you, you fucking arseholes. I hope you're proud."

None of them replied as they filed into the complex and it took all of Vicky's resolve to refrain from lashing out at them. She shared a look with Flynn, but they didn't speak to one another.

As the stragglers returned—an exhausted Serj among them—the entirety of Moira's community had turned to face the battle with the horde of diseased. When Vicky saw Moira, her entire frame locked tight.

Clearly consumed with panic, Moira stood—or rather, hid—behind her army as they battled the diseased.

A look at both Flynn and Serj and Vicky said, "I need to do this. That woman can't walk away."

A stoic nod from Flynn and he stepped forward.

"I need you on the door," Vicky said to him. "I need someone here on my side who'll let me back in when I return. I worry some of them will lock me out given half a chance." She looked inside and glared at Sharon.

For a moment, Flynn looked like he would contest Vicky's request. Instead, he dropped his shoulders with a sigh and nodded. "Just hurry up, yeah?"

Vicky took off through the long grass.

The closer Vicky got to the battle between Moira's community and the diseased, the more rancid the smell. The diseased's stench soured the air.

The long grass whipped at Vicky's midriff and made it hard to see the fallen bodies from the battle. However, when she got closer to them, the grass remained trampled from the fight and they were easy to avoid. She jumped several corpses in her way.

Moira—much like the people of her community—seemed more concerned with the diseased at that moment. The witch didn't even turn to face Vicky as she closed down on her.

As much as Vicky could have used her bat on the vicious woman, she reached around for the knife in the back of her belt and teased it free.

Just two steps separated the pair when Vicky raised the blade and yelled, "You fucking cunt!" She drove it into the side of Moira's head, knocking the bitch sideways from the blow, her long black hair whipping away from her as she fell.

Some of the people in Moira's community turned to look at

Vicky, but with their comrades falling around them, they quickly turned back to the threat in front of them.

Vicky didn't need another chance, so before anyone could register what had happened, she spun around and headed back to Home.

When Vicky returned to the flattened grass and the fallen people, she jumped over the downed bodies again, her lungs burning with the pain of trying to keep going.

Back at Home's entrance, Vicky looked at Flynn and the boy nodded at her. If his face presented an accurate representation of his mood, then he understood Vicky's need to go it alone with killing Moira. Out of breath and struggling to get it back, she nodded at Flynn. They'd done it.

Just before Vicky entered Home, Serj grabbed her arm and said, "Look."

Vicky turned to see one of their number coming back to the complex and she gasped. "Piotr?"

The large man ran with a heavy gait, his bulky frame clearly not designed for sprinting. As Vicky, Flynn, and Serj waited for the big man, Vicky's heart lifted. They might have had a beef, but Piotr had been a good friend.

When Piotr stopped about five metres short of Home's entrance, Vicky gasped. "What the *hell* are you doing?"

Piotr shook his head and looked from her to Flynn to Serj.

Dread tugged on Vicky's body as if the planet's gravitational pull had been turned up. Nausea rolled through her guts. She didn't need to see it to know the problem, but Piotr pulled his sleeve back anyway and showed them the bite. "Fuck," Vicky muttered.

Flynn cried out, "No! Piotr, please come back. We can fix it."

"No, you can't," the large Russian replied. "This is the end for me."

Tears ran down Flynn's cheeks and he shook his head. "No, it can't be. Piotr, please."

"I'm sorry, Flynn."

Grief stuck Vicky's words in her throat and she had to force them out. "Thank you," she said to Piotr. "Thank you for all you've done for Flynn. You've been great for him."

When Vicky looked at Flynn, she saw the boy seemed unable to speak through his grief.

A confused frown crushed Piotr's face as he also cried. "I'm sorry, Vicky."

"Don't be sorry; you didn't mean to get bitten."

Piotr looked like he wanted to say more. Instead, he shook his head and said, "I'm sorry." He then turned to face the battle on the other side of the meadow and ran towards the people from Moira's community.

Once Piotr had halved the distance between him and them, his right arm snapped away from him in a spasm. Clumsy in his movements, he spasmed again. Another snap away with his left arm, this time as if he'd been jabbed with electricity. His head tilted to one side. Another twitch and he roared.

Just as he jumped on the back of the pack, Vicky reached across and tugged on Flynn's arm.

Flynn might have looked like he didn't want to follow Vicky, but he didn't resist her pull either. Instead, he walked into Home with her, his form slumped, his head dropped.

Vicky pulled Home's large front door closed and slid the bolts across on the top and the bottom. The only sound remaining came from the ragged recovery of exhaustion as the people in the foyer pulled themselves together. Then she reached up and whacked the button to set the siren off.

The loud wail rang out, and when Vicky turned around, many of the people there stared at her. "I want to make sure no one gets away. If that wasn't all the diseased in the area, it soon will be. No way can those fuckers walk away from this. No way."

Chapter Sixty-Three

Vicky only realised Aaron had come up to Home's foyer when she moved over to one of the large windows and found herself standing next to him. As gaunt as ever, but much cleaner, he stood in one of Home's grey tracksuits. He'd washed his hair, shaved his face, and any trace of the stench of human waste had gone.

Outside, Moira's crowd were being torn apart by the diseased and more arrived at the back of the meadow, clearly in response to the siren.

A glassy sheen covered Aaron's hollow eyes and he spoke with a warble in his voice. "I never thought I'd get away from them. Stuck in that fucking prison, I couldn't *ever* see a way out."

To touch one of his razor-sharp shoulders made Vicky flinch, but she kept her hand there as she looked into the man's hollow stare. "You're safe now. She's gone for good."

"I saw what you did to her." And without another word, Aaron reached up across his chest and placed his hand over the back of Vicky's.

They stood in silence for a moment before they looked outside again. Vicky watched the diseased Piotr stalk the line of guards from Moira's community, clearly looking for one of them to attack. "Looks like slim pickings," she said, pushing the words through her grief. "Those on their feet all seem to be infected. Those on the ground are either turning or dead."

Several blinks later and tears ran freely down Vicky's cheeks as she kept her focus outside. The siren rang out as a wet pulse that spread out into the meadow. Regardless of how Piotr had made her feel when it came to Flynn, they'd lost a good and principled man. Home would be poorer for his absence. However, as much as she hated herself for thinking it, her secret had hopefully just died on the battlefield with him.

"Right," Vicky said as she wiped the tears from her eyes and sniffed against her running nose. "We need to check everyone for bites." She turned the siren off. "No one's getting any farther than here without being checked."

"Who the fuck made *you* boss?"

Vicky looked into the crowd to see Brian flanked by Sharon and Dan. He glared at her with his usual hatred.

Exhaustion had lifted Vicky's emotions to the surface and she couldn't hold back. "Fuck you, Brian."

Several of the people in the foyer gasped and silence descended on the place.

"You're a fucking piece of shit, you know that? You, you, and you"—she pointed at Sharon and Dan too—"left me for dead out there when I needed your help. Stuart died rescuing me. He wouldn't have needed to if you'd done the right thing."

"And you'd know about doing the right thing, would you?"

"What the fuck's *that* supposed to mean?"

A twisted expression of disgust and Brian didn't respond for a few seconds. He then said, "Stuart died because he was too fucking loyal to you. He died because he was *stupid*."

The space went from silent to a vacuum. Before Vicky could say anything, Serj nudged his way through the press of people and grabbed her shoulder so he could drag her closer and whisper in her ear, "Don't do this now."

Vicky turned her back on Brian, Dan, and Sharon and kept her voice low as she leaned close to Serj. "Why?"

The gravity of his stare cut straight to Vicky's core and he spoke so only she heard him. "You don't want this discussion here, not in front of everyone."

Fuck! Vicky looked into Serj's dark eyes and her heart sank. They knew. It must have been why Piotr apologised before he turned. They fucking knew.

A quick glance around and Vicky picked Flynn out of the crowd. So consumed with his grief for Piotr, he didn't seem too engaged with the drama. Better it stayed that way. If he found out that Piotr had repeated what he'd blurted out, then he might not be able to live with himself.

Vicky turned back to Serj and whispered, "Okay. Let's talk later."

Serj nodded. "You go and rest and we'll sort out whatever needs to be sorted out. How about we meet up after dinner? I'll make this lot hold off until tomorrow."

They would take her to task. A deep breath and Vicky nodded slowly at him.

"Flynn," Serj called over to the boy, "I need your help

checking people for bites before we let them in."

A look back at Home's residents and Vicky saw a very different reaction to her than what she'd previously seen. How many people already knew? What would they do to her because of it?

Vicky's head spun as she stumbled off. Finally, after all these years, the past had caught up with her.

Chapter Sixty-Four

Vicky returned to her room, her head spinning from a mixture of fatigue and fear. Piotr *had* told the people of Home what Flynn had blurted out. In their minds, she was responsible for the virus's release. Most people in Home feared her. Many openly hated her. None of them would listen to the truth of it. Not that the truth would make her look much better. Were it not for her, then Brendan or Oscar or whatever the fucking prick's name was wouldn't have been able to do what he did. The people would want justice and who could blame them?

There were many things she could have done with what would more than likely be her last day in Home. But once she lay on her bed, her body seemed to treble in weight and she couldn't move.

Not that she slept, she simply stared up at the white ceiling, her eyes on fire from blinking so infrequently. A low-level buzz of exhaustion ran through her body. It sat deep in her muscles, and for the next few hours she felt as if she'd never get up again.

The activity outside Vicky's room told her the dinner shift had started.

It took another hour or so for Vicky to finally will herself to get up and head to the canteen. Wobbly on her weak legs when she stood up, her hunger ate away at her like a parasite. Otherwise, she probably would have remained in her room.

***

When Vicky got to the canteen, the place seemed busier than she'd seen it in a long time. Maybe the camaraderie of war had pulled the community closer together. Maybe they needed comfort as they grieved for those lost on the battlefield.

The monitors showed images of the diseased outside and the sun setting on the horizon. There seemed to be hundreds of the fuckers wandering aimlessly as if in hope of finding something to attack. Vicky didn't watch the screens for long. She'd seen more than enough already.

Not all of the faces in the canteen stared at her, but many did. One particularly packed table had Brian, Dan, and Sharon at it. All three of them and all of the people around them glared at Vicky. They blamed her and they probably should.

If the looks were anything to go by, plenty of people knew what Vicky had done. Hopefully Serj had been good to his word and kept that from Flynn. If he found out, he'd work out they knew because of him. Not that he should blame himself, he didn't do anything wrong, but he wouldn't see it like that.

Vicky saw Flynn in the corner at a table by himself. On her way over to him, she picked up a tray of stew.

***

Despite having the taste of meat, Vicky found no trace of it when she ate the vegetable broth. For a few minutes neither her nor Flynn spoke. From repeated glances at the boy, she struggled to see a way to get through his grief. "He was a good man," she finally said.

"I know." Flynn's response snapped back at her like the crack of a whip and he continued to stare at his food.

"He'll be sorely missed."

"Don't give me that."

"What do you mean?"

Flynn looked up at her, his eyes narrowed. "You won't miss him. You were jealous of him. I could see that."

"I wasn't jealous." Vicky looked around at that moment to see many people still watched her. Hostility emanated from their dark glares.

"Why did you look at him like you did, then?"

"I never resented Piotr for being there for you. I loved that you had someone there to confide in. It just made me sad that I couldn't be that person. I knew I was always too overbearing."

The angry scowl on Flynn's face softened and he sighed. Tears glazed his eyes. "Yeah, you were."

"I'm sorry. Please know it comes from a place of love, however misguided."

Flynn nodded. "Piotr always said that to me."

The comment made Vicky's eyes itch with tears, but she blinked them away. This moment shouldn't be about her. She needed to make sure Flynn would be okay. "You're a brave young man, you know that?"

The frown returned and Flynn didn't reply.

"You have good morals and you're a strong leader. You're a survivor and people like you. You will always be like a son to me, Flynn. I'm sorry if that's made you feel awkward, but know I love you without condition."

"I know," Flynn said, his attention back on his dinner. His lip buckled and he cleared his throat before he said, "Look, I want to go and lie down."

It didn't matter how many times Vicky swallowed, she couldn't clear the lump in her throat. A nod at Flynn and she said okay, despite a desire to hold on to him and never let go. "Take care of yourself, okay? Never forget how much I love you."

The same confused frown returned and Flynn nodded. "I *know*, Vicky." He rolled his eyes, and for the first time in what felt like months, he reached across and held her hand, his dark and watery stare looking straight into hers. Maybe he understood what was about to happen, even if he didn't realise it.

After he'd let go, Vicky's hand turned cold as if longing for one last touch, one last moment of affection to take with her. Whatever happened, she wouldn't be able to stay in Home. She watched him leave the canteen at a slow trudge. Tears dampened her cheeks and dripped onto her lap to see him leave her life. A knot tied in her guts and she pushed her tray of food away from her. It didn't matter who looked at her anymore. They could fuck off and die for all she cared. Fuck them.

Once Flynn had left, Vicky got up and left the canteen too.

***

By the time Vicky returned to her room, she couldn't see for tears. It took several attempts for her to reach the door handle to get into the place.

Vicky jumped when she entered and found Serj waiting for her.

A twist of apology turned his features and he said, "I'm sorry, Vicky. I wish I could make it work so you could stay here. I'll miss you more than you know."

"I understand," Vicky said. "Just let me do it on my terms, yeah?"

Serj drew a deep inhale and his cheeks puffed out when he let it go. He didn't respond to her.

Chapter Sixty-Five

Flynn woke up and ached all over. The battle the day before had taken it out of him and he missed Piotr like he'd lost a part of himself. Vicky had gone all weird on him and he needed the big Russian man now more than ever. But he had cleared the air with her at least. Maybe they could find a way to get on again. She'd been such a pain in his arse for the longest time.

Although he didn't want to get up, Flynn forced himself to sit in his bed. The voice of his fallen comrade, Piotr, echoed through his mind. *Keep going, Flynn. You need to keep going.*

Before Flynn could do much else, he saw a piece of paper folded up on his duvet. When he picked it up and unfolded it, he saw Vicky's writing.

Dear Flynn,

I've chosen to go now. The fact is, I can't stay here after all the shit that's happened. I'm not good for the mood of this place, and now Moira's gone, I'm not needed. You've seen the effect my presence has on people. A lot of them blame me for the war with Moira, and maybe they're right to. The fact is, I can't stay here any longer. Don't try to follow, you'll never find me, and I've got a good lead on you already.

I want you to know you're the bravest person I've ever met. You're so loyal and I know you'd come after me if you could, so please trust me when I say you'll NEVER find me. You need to make a go of things in Home and I don't want to get in the way of that. Things are on the up for you, so stay there and realise the greatness you have inside. Serj needs a new deputy and you're a warrior more than fit for the task.

Flynn's pulse pounded through his skull and his head spun. He continued to read.

I love you more than you'll ever know. I know we've butted heads, but it never once diluted how I feel about you. If you feel angry towards anyone and how they treated me, please let that go. I would make the same decisions and accept the same consequences all over again. To blame the people around you will eat you from the inside out. The truth is, the only person to blame here is me. I'm responsible for this mess, so I'm taking myself away from it. I don't want to jeopardise your future.

If there's one thing we're on this planet for, it's to make sure we do everything we can to make the next generation better than we've been. You're a thousand times the person I could ever be, so take that and burn bright with it. Help future generations make this world shine again.

Things will get better as long as there's people like you in the world. You'll find happiness beyond this. Know that's all we'll ever want for you. Your mum, your dad, and me. We all want you to live your life to its fullest. Be strong and walk with the love of generations in your heart. Make this world your own and don't be afraid to show everyone the warrior within.

As I walk in the shadows, I'll have the light of my love for you in my heart. Be strong and burn bright.

Love always,

Vicky XXX

By the time he'd finished reading the letter, Flynn's hands shook, wobbling the sheet of paper. The grief for Piotr trebled to know Vicky had gone too. And she'd *chosen* to go. Chosen to leave him when he needed her most …

Epilogue

THE PREVIOUS EVENING

After Vicky had written Flynn a letter, she folded it and gave it to Serj. "Make sure he gets it."

Serj nodded.

Vicky knew what had to happen. Whether she agreed with it or not, she had to accept the way of things around here. No one would forgive her for the virus, and why should they? After she'd taken all of her weapons out and thrown them on her bed, she offered her wrists to Serj to bind.

A glassy stare and Serj shook his head.

***

"This has to happen," Brian said when Vicky arrived in the foyer with Serj. The vicious man stood next to Sharon, Dan, and several other people from Home.

"I always knew you were a cunt," Brian added, "but to know you're the reason this fucking virus happened."

"I didn't *create* it."

"Did you or did you not help release it upon the world?"

Instead of answering, Vicky stared at the floor and sighed.

"Exactly. How can you expect the people here to be happy with you staying when you're the reason their loved ones are dead?"

"Just fucking get on with it, yeah?" Vicky said.

A flash of anger snapped across Brian's face before he drew a deep breath, stepped forwards, and cable tied her hands. "Not that I'm inclined to grant them, but do you have any last requests?"

"Just make sure Flynn thinks I've gone. I want him to be safe here, and if he thinks I've left him and don't want to be found, he'll stay. If he knows you found out about what I did and that you've sentenced me, he'll leave. He's only a boy. He's done nothing wrong and shouldn't be punished for *my* mistakes."

Cruelty twisted Brian's features, and before he could answer, Serj said, "I'll make sure that happens. Also, we *don't* use the alarm tonight."

A few of the group looked at Serj.

"We don't need to," Serj said. "There are enough diseased out there. We don't need to make a big show of it. Whatever you think of Vicky and her past, she fought hard in this war and she's the reason we still live here."

"The war wouldn't have ever *happened* were it not for her," Sharon said. "My kids would still be alive."

Serj shook his head and didn't reply.

As much as Vicky wanted to be calm in the face of her own end, she drew deep breaths, but they did little to settle her fluttering heart. A hot throb ran through her hands from where

Brian had fastened the cable tightly around her wrists.

"I promise you," Serj said, his eyes tearing up again as he put his arm around Vicky, "Flynn will *never* know what happened here. If anyone tries to tell him, they'll be out the door next."

"Thank you," Vicky said, her grief cutting off her words.

On her way to the front door, Vicky glanced out of one of the large windows. Scores of diseased milled about in the darkness. At least it would be quick.

The top lock on the door snapped free from where Brian released it. The second made the same loud *crack*. One final angry glare at Vicky and he said, "You'd best get the fuck out with no nonsense."

Just before Brian opened the door, Serj wrapped Vicky in a tight hug. The man smelled of soap and Vicky breathed in her final moments of human contact.

After Serj had pulled away from her, Vicky nodded at him, her world blurred through her tears. "Please look after Flynn."

Serj nodded back, clearly unable to speak.

The hinges creaked as Brian opened the door, and before Vicky knew it, Dan and Sharon grabbed an arm each and shoved her out.

Two steps through the long grass and Vicky fell forward. The pain of hitting the ground clattered through her knees and up her body.

As she kneeled there, surrounded by tall grass, she looked at the ground and listened to the stampede close in on her. It drew closer and closer until it got to within a few metres and she looked up.

"Piotr," she gasped as she stared into the bleeding eyes of the large Russian man. Of course he would be the alpha.

But it wasn't Piotr. Piotr had left that body the second the virus took him over.

The imposing form of the former guard dived down on Vicky, body slamming her and crushing the air from her lungs.

Pain ripped from Vicky's cheek. Excruciating fire radiated from the bite outwards.

The ground shook as more diseased closed in. The press of bodies quickly blocked out the light around her and several spots on her form lit up as more of the fuckers bit into her.

After a spike in her panic, the buzz of pain faded a little. Vicky's heart rate slowed. The blood loss made her dizzy as she lay there. She refused to look back. She wouldn't give the fuckers the satisfaction.

Every blink lasted slightly longer than the one before it as she lost her bearings. The heat from the fever and the press of bodies lifted sweat on her brow. Her eyes burned and she saw the world through a red tint. She thought of Flynn. Of the boy she loved more than anything in this life. She thought about … Who? What? She … she couldn't remember … The boy? His face. Rage swelled within her as if her blood boiled. She smelled the metallic reek of her spilled life force. Her blood. Their blood. The smell made her mouth water. She could almost taste it. Her teeth snapped together as she bit the air. She bit again, her pulse hammering. Where were they? Bite. She could smell them. Bite. She needed flesh. Bite …

Ends.

Would you like to be notified when I have a new release?
Join my mailing list for all of my updates here:

www.michaelrobertson.co.uk

Support the Author

Dear reader, as an independent author I don't have the resources of a huge publisher. If you like my work and would like to see more from me in the future, there are two things you can do to help: leaving a review, and a word-of-mouth referral.

Releasing a book takes many hours and hundreds of dollars. I love to write, and would love to continue to do so. All I ask is that you leave an Amazon review. It shows other readers that you've enjoyed the book and will encourage them to give it a try too. The review can be just one sentence, or as long as you like.

Other Works Available by Michael Robertson

The Shadow Order - Available Now:

New Reality: Truth - Available now for FREE:

Crash - Available now for FREE:

Rat Run - Available Now:

For my other titles and mailing list - go to www.michaelrobertson.co.uk

About The Author

Like most children born in the seventies, Michael grew up with Star Wars in his life. An obsessive watcher of the films, and an avid reader from an early age, he found himself taken over with stories whenever he let his mind wander.

Those stories had to come out.
He hopes you enjoy reading his books as much as he does writing them.

Michael loves to travel when he can. He has a young family, who are his world, and when he's not reading, he enjoys walking so he can dream up more stories.

To be notified of Michael's future books, please sign up at www.michaelrobertson.co.uk

Email at: subscribers@michaelrobertson.co.uk

Follow me on facebook at –
https://www.facebook.com/MichaelRobertsonAuthor

Twitter at – @MicRobertson

Google Plus at –
https://plus.google.com/u/0/113009673177382863155/posts

OTHER AUTHORS UNDER THE SHIELD OF

SIXTH CYCLE

Nuclear war has destroyed human civilization.
Captain Jake Phillips wakes into a dangerous new world, where he finds the remaining fragments of the population living in a series of strongholds, connected across the country. Uneasy alliances have maintained their safety, but things are about to change. — Discovery **leads to danger.** — Skye Reed, a tracker from the Omega stronghold, uncovers a threat that could spell the end for their fragile society. With friends and enemies revealing truths about the past, she will need to decide who to trust. — **Sixth Cycle** is a gritty post-apocalyptic story of survival and adventure.

Darren Wearmouth - Carl Sinclair

DEAD ISLAND: Operation Zulu

Ten years after the world was nearly brought to its knees by a zombie Armageddon, there is a race for the antidote! On a remote Caribbean island, surrounded by a horde of hungry living dead, a team of American and Australian commandos must rescue the Antidotes' scientist. Filled with zombies, guns, Russian bad guys, shady government types, serial killers and elevator muzak. Dead Island is an action packed blood soaked horror adventure.

Allen Gamboa

INVASION OF THE DEAD SERIES

This is the first book in a series of nine, about an ordinary bunch of friends, and their plight to survive an apocalypse in Australia. — Deep beneath defense headquarters in the Australian Capital Territory, the last ranking Army chief and a brilliant scientist struggle with answers to the collapse of the world, and the aftermath of an unprecedented virus. Is it a natural mutation, or does the infection contain — more sinister roots? — One hundred and fifty miles away, five friends returning from a month-long camping trip slowly discover that death has swept through the country. What greets them in a gradual revelation is an enemy beyond compare. — Armed with dwindling ammunition, the friends must overcome their disagreements, utilize their individual skills, and face unimaginable horrors as they battle to reach their hometown…

Owen Baillie

WHISKEY TANGO FOXTROT

Alone in a foreign land. The radio goes quiet while on convoy in Afghanistan, a lost patrol alone in the desert. With his unit and his home base destroyed, Staff Sergeant Brad Thompson suddenly finds himself isolated and in command of a small group of men trying to survive in the Afghan wasteland. **Every turn leads to danger**

The local population has been afflicted with an illness that turns them into rabid animals. They pursue him and his men at every corner and stop. Struggling to hold his team together and unite survivors, he must fight and evade his way to safety.

A fast paced zombie war story like no other.

W.J. Lundy

ZOMBIE RUSH

New to the Hot Springs PD Lisa Reynolds was not all that welcomed by her coworkers especially those who were passed over for the position. It didn't matter, her thirty days probation ended on the same day of the Z-poc's arrival. Overnight the world goes from bad to worse as thousands die in the initial onslaught. National Guard and regular military unit deployed the day before to the north leaves the city in mayhem. All directions lead to death until one unlikely candidate steps forward with a plan. A plan that became an avalanche raging down the mountain culminating in the salvation or destruction of them all.

Joseph Hansen

THE GATHERING HORDE

The most ambitious terrorist plot ever undertaken is about to be put into motion, releasing an unstoppable force against humanity. Ordinary people – A group of students celebrating the end of the semester, suburban and rural families – are about to themselves in the center of something that threatens the survival of the human species. As they battle the dead – and the living – it's going to take every bit of skill, knowledge and luck for them to survive in Zed's World.

Rich Baker

THE FORGOTTEN LAND

Sergeant Steve Golburn, an Australian Special Air Service veteran, is tasked with a dangerous mission in Iraq, deep behind enemy lines. When Steve's five man SAS patrol inadvertently spark a time portal, they find themselves in 10th century Viking Denmark. A place far more dangerous and lawless than modern Iraq. Join the SAS patrol on this action adventure into the depths of not only a hostile land, far away from the support of the Allied front line, but into another world…another time.

Keith McArdle

<<<<>>>>

Printed in Great Britain
by Amazon